RL 5.0

true confessions of a heartless girl

Also by Martha Brooks

true confessions
of a heartless girl

MARTHA BROOKS

MELANIE KROUPA BOOKS • FARRAR STRAUS GIROUX

The author acknowledges the generous assistance of the Canada Council for the Arts and—as always—the fine editorial team of Melanie Kroupa, of Farrar, Straus and Giroux, New York, and Shelley Tanaka, of Groundwood Books, Toronto.

Copyright © 2003 by Martha Brooks
All rights reserved
First published in Canada by Groundwood Books / Douglas & McIntyre Ltd.
First American edition, 2003
Printed in the United States of America
Designed by Nancy Goldenberg
7   9   10   8   6

Library of Congress Cataloging-in-Publication Data
Brooks, Martha, 1944–
    True confessions of a heartless girl : a novel / by Martha Brooks.—
1st American ed.
        p.   cm.
    Summary: A confused seventeen-year-old girl, a single mother and her young son, two elderly women, and a sad and lonely man, with their own individual tragedies to bear, come together in a small Manitoba town and find a way to a better future.
    ISBN 0-374-37806-1
    [1. Interpersonal relations—Fiction.   2. City and town life—Fiction.
3. Manitoba—Fiction.   4. Canada—Fiction.]   I. Title.

PZ7.B7975 Tt 2003
[Fic]—dc21

                                                                2002072461

This book is gratefully dedicated to the circles of women who grace my life, who nurture me daily with their physical presence, or in memory, or in the shared ancestral sisterhood of dreaming.

The American novelist John Gardner, I think it was, said there are, really, only two plot lines: a stranger rides into town, and a stranger rides out of town.

—William Least Heat-Moon
PrairyErth

part one

THE STRANGER

1

The July storm moved down the valley, rumbling around either side of the hills and Pembina Lake. It was ten o'clock in the evening and veins of light flashed across the sky, an immense and rounded womb. Inside the belly of this Goddess, as the hard rain fell, farmers pulled their mowers out of the ditches, townspeople ran through growing puddles to their homes, women closed bedroom windows, mopped the ledges, covered their sleeping children.

Dolores Harper called up her oldest friend in the world, Mary Reed, to ask if she'd like a little company, and Mary, celebrating the impending birth of her first great-grandchild, said she'd put on the kettle and they could play a little penny poker and that way pass the evening until they got the news.

Lynda Bradley, proprietor of the Molly Thorvaldson Café, saw her last customer out the door and, before turning the Open sign to Closed, began to do the cash. Her five-year-old son, Seth, upstairs on the second floor of the hundred-year-old brick building, dozed in front of the TV, a half-eaten chicken leg still clutched in his fist.

At first Lynda did her best to ignore the truck pulling up to the door of her café. Its lights flashed briefly through the windows, then died. A throbbing ache at her temples and right behind her eyeballs had been gathering power all afternoon as the barometric pressure dropped. Now all she hoped was that whoever was out there would have a change of mind, disappear into the night, and leave her alone. She thought about going to the door and turning over the Open sign, but it had to be some neighbor, some farmer, some regular, and then of course she'd never hear the end of it. So she tallied up the cash and waited. If they wanted to come in, why didn't they just do that, instead of sitting out there in the dark?

She went to the window and peered past the rivulets snaking drearily down the glass. She couldn't see a thing. Exasperated, she went to the door, opened it wide, and stood there until the driver of the truck, a small person, a stranger as it turned out, got the hint, jumped down from the cab, and ran through the puddles past her into the café.

Lynda closed the door and went back inside. The girl, now sitting shivering on one of the stools, nervously flattened drenched wisps of badly cut blond hair, looked Lynda's way, and then back at the long shiny counter.

"I'm closing soon," Lynda said. Something in this young stranger's eyes, a kind of dark pleading, made her stop short of saying that, in fact, she *was* closed.

"Can I have a coffee?" A sharp intake of breath.

"Sure." Lynda poured the dregs of the coffee, which had been fresh over an hour ago, into a mug and set it in front of the girl. She stood back, watching as skinny trembling fingers (two silver rings on each hand) broke open four containers of cream, dumped them in, then added three heaping spoonfuls of sugar.

"White death." A rueful smile at Lynda. Then, stopping just short of spoonful number four, she stirred the sweet sandy sludge.

"So where're you coming from?" Making cheerful conversation, the polite thing to do even at the end of the day, when Lynda's ankles and wrists were throbbing.

But the girl ignored this, looking around, taking in the wallpaper (Lynda knew it looked like a depressing mistake) and the heavy wooden booths along the west wall, where Joe Hartman, the former owner and also her mother's sometime boyfriend, used to sit at the end of every day, the fried chip smell still clinging to him.

Finally the girl spoke. "I don't know where the hell I am."

"You are in Pembina Lake," Lynda replied curtly. "Town of, to be precise. Lake itself being down at the end of the main drag."

No response. She just hunched over her mug and blew on tiny clouds of rising steam, every so often flicking an apprehensive glance toward the door.

Lynda tried again. "Quite the storm. Must be hard to see where you're going, back out there on the highway."

White teeth chattered and clicked against the rim of the cup. "Some asshole almost ran me off the road." A pause. "Is there a motel in this town?"

"Afraid not. Our one and only was torched by a twelve-year-old arsonist. Last October. No one has thought to rebuild it since."

The shoulders sagged. There were ragged moons of metallic orange on her fingernails—probably the remains of a home manicure done with cheap shiny polish, the kind that curdles quickly in the bottle. She looked to be around seventeen—a familiar age. Lynda was transported back to the English class she had taught, it now seemed a lifetime ago, at a high school in Winnipeg's inner city. There a haunted look could mean anything: alcoholic parents, hunger, an abusive boyfriend, drugs, troubles with the law, the old downward spiral. Fear clung to this girl as well, and this, too, was familiar—as though she had done something wrong and was a breath away from being caught.

Then Lynda thought about the truck as the girl once again glanced toward the door. Maybe she should call the police. "Look," she said, "I've got a real bad headache and the feeling that you are in some kind of trouble. So I'll just cut to the chase here and ask straight out. Are you? In some kind of trouble?"

The girl gave a little sickened movement of her head, a sudden slackening of her dry lower lip. Lynda knew right then that there *was* trouble, knew it with a feeling that told her if she was smart she'd just let this kid get back in the truck and get swallowed up by the storm. Life would continue in the same old way. Then she thought back to the day that she herself had been in trouble, the day she first arrived back in town—three and a half years ago, during the misery of a February blizzard. Dolores took her in, her little boy, too; she didn't have to do that. Nobody had to do anything; it wasn't a requirement in this life that you burden yourself with somebody else's baggage. It wasn't necessary to lay yourself open for more trouble than you already owned.

Lynda drew in a long breath, looked at the bedraggled creature who had landed in her café, and said with a terrible sinking feeling, "So why don't you tell me about it?"

2

All night the rain kept falling, filling up the gutters, swirling down little ridges, gathering in glistening pools, drenching mallard ducks and their offspring nestled under fronds of pale green meadow rue in the oak woods that skirted the lake.

Dolores Harper and Mary Reed, still waiting for news of grandson Ronnie's firstborn child, sat in Mary's kitchen with the seventeen potted plants, many of them flourishing in shiny tin cans, all jammed together on two paint-blistered windowsills. They were finished with penny poker—Dolores was one hundred thirty-eight cents richer—and they had moved on to discussing Lynda Bradley.

"I pray for that girl every day," said Dolores. "I ask the Creator to send her somebody nice. Doesn't have to be handsome. Or even so young. It's what she needs."

"What our Lynda *needs*," said Mary, "is something to wake her up! Girl's got what—five degrees?"

Dolores stuck up two fingers.

"She could be doing something. She's making hamburgers. *Hamburgers!* And they taste bad. Gawdawful. Packaged kind. No wonder people have gone from calling it the M.T. to the *Empty* Café behind her back. Well? Don't give me that look. It's true. What has she got? A pretty good coffee crowd. And they'll buy the odd meal to help her out—that's how people are. And the cottagers coming around three months out of every twelve. And the Saturday morning pancake breakfasts have been real popular—now that you're there to give her a hand. But that's peanuts. People are driving *twenty minutes* to get a real meal up at Willow Point. Can you explain to me what is wrong with her head?"

Dolores opened her mouth to say something, shot a look at her friend, then closed it again. In the old days she would have started up an argument. Lately she just couldn't find the heart.

Mary threw up her hands. "Worst thing Joe Hartman could have done was to die and leave her that place. Like he owed her something? Please. Now she figures she'll settle into her misery and hide out from life like everybody else in this town."

Was she trying to pick a fight? Dolores sat there quietly, not taking the bait, her mind drifting back to her own terrible days of a year ago. What did Mary know about anything? Had she lost her only child? She had plenty of daughters. Not to mention grandchildren. And here was a first great-grandchild about to be born.

Mary leaned in and tried again. "And there's another thing. That boy of hers . . ."

"Far too spoiled," said Dolores, unable to keep herself from finishing the sentence.

Mary sat back, elated. "Well, he is!" she crowed. "Five years old and still treated like a baby. She hangs on to him for dear life. It's unhealthy. She's going to stunt his growth. You just watch."

Dolores reached for the berry jam she and Mary had made together last fall, from crabapples no one could ever keep up with, from drooping masses of chokecherries that had rapidly filled their pails up on Tiger Lily hill. That was just before Mary stopped driving her car, for no good reason. Now they never went anywhere. Lately they just seemed to be going through the motions of their friendship. The old closeness was gone. They hardly ever laughed anymore. They used to laugh until they peed themselves, just like a couple of kids.

Dolores sighed. With a heavy heart she dug into the jam, then spooned it onto a rectangle of the pan-fried bannock she'd brought over to share with her friend. She thought to herself that Lynda was bringing Seth up just right. Children needed time to just be children. Life was short. Even shorter for some. Good thing we didn't know what the future held. Good thing we were spared that.

At that point the telephone rang. Ronnie's wife, Clarissa, had just delivered a baby girl into the world, an angry, red-faced, screaming treasure they had already named Caitlin Louise.

Dolores should probably have stayed a little longer—to help her friend celebrate the blessed event—but she couldn't stop thinking about how she would never hold any grandchildren or great-grandchildren of her own in her arms. Without another word, she picked up her Pembina Valley Trail Busters cap, put it

on her head, and left Mary, her face glowing, still talking on the
phone to Ronnie.

3

When you helped somebody, right away you were responsible for
that person. And things always followed for which you were never
prepared. Like that half-grown Labrador pup last summer—that
nobody, of course, knew anything about. One thing led to another, and now, three hundred dollars' worth of shots, spaying,
dog food, dog toys, and other incidentals later, Tessie practically
owned the place. Customers would even protest if she kicked her
back outside after she had sneaked in on hot days. They'd look at
her as if she was sentencing her to heatstroke. There was just no
winning in a situation where you took that kind of responsibility.

But Lynda made up the cot anyway, in the cramped spare bedroom that doubled as her musty-smelling office, opening the
window that looked down on the street and the glistening rain-
slicked truck still parked where the girl had left it a couple of
hours before. She lifted a stack of unpaid bills from the top of her
desk and felt that all-too-familiar wave of defeat before stuffing
them into a drawer.

"Bathroom's down the hall," she instructed the girl, who stood
waiting sullenly near the door. "I'm going to put my son to bed
now. Then I'm going to bed myself. I suggest you do the same."

Later, as the building settled and the damp night seeped

through the windows, the sleepless girl got up in the darkness and stole into the living room, flopping down on the sofa where the boy had been lying. She felt along the seat covers for the TV remote, but instead her hand came across a slimy gnawed-on chicken leg. She flipped it with a disgusted grunt onto the coffee table. It hit the wooden surface and made a hollow sound.

The dog appeared like a shadow, then sat in front of her, tail thumping hard against the floor. "Piss off," hissed the girl. But the dog wasn't leaving. So she quickly leaned forward, picked up the leg, and hurled it at the animal, who leaped straight up and caught it, then slumped with a contented sigh to the floor. A bolt of lightning flashed outside and brightened the room, illuminating the dog's face, her teeth, as she cracked the bone into arrowlike shards.

4

At seventy-six, Dolores Harper still had the energy of a sixty-year-old. And she liked helping Lynda at the Molly Thorvaldson Café every Saturday. It was something to do and it kept her spirits up.

A year ago, when her daughter died of leukemia at the age of thirty-six—same age Lynda was now—she missed a Saturday. When she got back, Del Armstrong, a bachelor farmer in his early fifties, shyly presented her with a sympathy card as she brought him three eggs, over easy, and the pancake special.

"Sorry for your loss," he said.

She stood beside him, stunned and pleased and sad.

"Read it later," he said, eyeing the card in its blue envelope. Then he added gruffly, almost in a whisper, "Lost my big brother, Danny—be thirty-four years ago this week."

"I remember Danny," Dolores said softly.

"Guess you do," said Del.

She'd put her hand on his shoulder—something she should have done years ago. Everybody remembered Danny, the brother who had drowned right here in this valley's precious lake. It was a local tragedy. She thought back to Del after it happened, how his youth got wasted on booze—before he discovered AA and workaholism and, down at the beach, that new addition he was building for Danny's barely lived-in cottage.

Back in the kitchen, she'd read, through her tears, a quote written in Del's thin spidery hand:

> *The land knows what its people know*
> *Time keeps slipping by*
> *The seasons and the heartbreak*
> *Gone in the blink of an eye*
> *—Lyleton Montgomery, cowboy poet*

She'd tucked it into her apron pocket and didn't show it to anyone, not even Lynda.

Then, later in that terrible month, Lynda presented her with a pink sweatshirt purchased in Winnipeg. Silk-screened in big block letters across the front was: OLDEST FIRST NATIONS WAIT-

RESS IN MANITOBA. Emblazoned across the back was her other claim to fame: MEDDLING FOR JESUS. It was a powerful shirt. And its sentiments were meant to be shared. Besides, it made her laugh and lightened her heart. Dolores wore it to Lynda's every Saturday, even on the hottest days.

This morning she left home a little earlier than usual to walk along the lake that swished and sashayed after the rain just like a sparkling green lady, washing up pink stones or, if you looked real close, the odd arrowhead, or scraper, or point, or the smoothed satiny section of a buffalo bone so old it had turned the color of pale milky tea. The rain always swept in lovely gifts. Some she would pick up with a little prayer, and others give back to nature.

Several minutes later she was in town, walking along the short main street: the Co-op gas station, the post office, Mildred's Hair Place, the Community Hall, Olifant and Son Lumber—out of business for six years but the buildings were still up for sale—Pembina Lake Credit Union, the abandoned crumbling structure that had once housed Sandee's Bakery and before then the Chinese café (where that old man hanged himself from the basement ceiling rafters in 1956, another local tragedy), Shore's Groceries, and, right across from it, the Molly Thorvaldson Café (which, through a hundred years of ups and downs, many owners, and many names, had always been a café).

It was close to seven o'clock when she arrived. She let herself in with the spare key. Once inside, she could hear Lynda already in the back, mixing up the batter for their Saturday morning special. She left the door open to let some of that sweet-smelling, rain-washed, early morning air come in through the screen. Then she walked to the back and into the kitchen.

Lynda turned from the big metal mixing bowl. Her skin had a particular glow this morning—reminding Dolores of that reddish-blond Celtic singer, Loreena McKennitt, whom Lynda was so fond of listening to. She had that same carelessly beautiful gold-hued quality—the kind of woman Raymond would have described as "a real humdinger."

Raymond. She missed him, too. There were just too many angels up there now. She sighed. Raymond would forever and always be the one great love of her life in spite of the fact that, as a husband, he had also been a pain in the ass to try and get along with.

"Morning, Lynda," she said. "Whose truck is parked outside?"

"Last night," said Lynda, "in the middle of that bad storm? Young girl drives up and comes in for coffee just as I'm trying to close." The spoon clinked rapidly against the sides of the bowl. She stopped, used her wrist to push back a lock of curly hair that had sprung from her ponytail, then returned to beating the batter. "You wouldn't believe this kid, Dolores. She is so messed up. I couldn't get a straight story out of her. Felt like I was back teaching at R. G. McGrath."

"So you let her stay the night," said Dolores, shaking her head. *"A complete stranger."*

"Yes, I let her stay the night," Lynda said defensively. "She was lost. It was late. The weather was awful. And of course I felt responsible."

"Of course," said Dolores, softening. Lynda, for all her smart-ness, felt responsible for everything. Probably would never have left that horrible husband of hers, that leech of a no-good bum, if he hadn't also turned out to be violent. Well, they should all get down on their knees in thankfulness that she did leave him. "Where is she now?" she asked.

"I made up the cot in my office. She's up there, sleeping."

"Then let her sleep. When she wakes we'll feed her up good. After that, if you want me to, I'll have a talk with her."

"I shouldn't bother you with this."

"It's no bother," Dolores replied quickly. And she meant it. It's just that today she would really have to work up to it.

"I sure would appreciate that. You have a way of making people tell the truth. You just seem to do it with no effort at all."

"It's a gift from the Higher Powers," Dolores told her firmly. "I can't take the credit." But her heart lifted just a little.

5

Customers always began to roll in for the Saturday morning spe-cial around eight o'clock. By now Lynda was frying bacon, flip-ping pancakes, mixing juice. She left the kitchen to pour water for the coffee. Instantly the fragrant liquid, which never tasted as good as it smelled, began to bubble and hiss down into the wait-ing glass pots.

This morning, rangy Del Armstrong, cowboy hat perched on

the back of his head, was the first one through the door. He took off his hat when he saw her, blushed, avoided her gaze, and quickly disappeared inside his own little world.

She listened with one ear as he told Dolores, "I need to stoke up good. Errands to run. Over at Brandon."

This was his way of saying that he'd have the same thing he'd ordered last Saturday. And the Saturday before that.

"And what are you picking up in the city today?" Dolores asked him.

"Lumber supplies. Building a lower deck. After haying's done."

"Still working away on Danny's old cottage?"

"Yup."

"Gonna be nice when you're all done," she said. "But of course the joy is in the planning."

She followed Lynda back to the kitchen and said in a low voice, "I never knew anybody to spend so much time and money on a place they hardly ever stay at. Well, I guess it keeps him going. We all need something."

Lynda went back to the stove, flipped over some pancakes, drained the bacon, started three eggs for Del, and said dispirit-edly, "Seth, stop feeding that dog from your spoon."

"Something's wrong, Mom," said Seth, pushing the spoon into the corner of Tessie's mouth, using it to try to lever her lip. "She doesn't *want* to eat."

The dog slumped to the floor and rolled her goofy eyes at Lynda, who suddenly laughed.

The girl from last night came down the back stairs and entered the kitchen. Disheveled, her blond hair now dry but sticking out every which way, she regarded the family scene for a moment, then slunk over to the corner table by the window.

"Hi," Seth said. "I'm trying to feed my dog." He laid his hand on the animal's head. "Are you sick, Tessie?"

The girl yawned, folding bare arms across her thin chest, and then shivered. She wore a blue T-shirt and low-riding dark green pants.

"You can pat her if you like. Are you staying for a while? We could go swimming. My best friend used to come with me but she moved away."

He looked hopefully at the girl, who now had a strange expression. Her face was red and sweaty. She went quickly into the little bathroom just off the kitchen and shut the door fast. He could hear her in there making loud choking sounds like she was crying or throwing up or maybe both.

His mother shook her head at this, looking the same way she looked when he did something very bad. Like the *worst* time: He'd found Del Armstrong's watch lying under the table where it had fallen out of the pocket of the big man's jeans. It was the old-fashioned windup kind. He loved the way it sounded. He felt like a giant looking into its face, because it had a gold second hand that was shaped like the smallest stalk of wheat in the world.

Even though he knew that Del was worried, and had asked if anybody had found the watch, he'd kept it for a long time without telling. Until it started to give him bad dreams. Auntie Dolores, with her eyes as kind as Jesus—who could search out a lie, even when you tried hard not to think it—had made him confess. He wondered what this girl had done. He wondered what could be worse than stealing somebody's gold watch.

The girl finally came out of the bathroom. Just as she sank into a chair at the table, Auntie Dolores walked back to the kitchen and came over to them, leaned down her face—her skin soft as an old nightie—and kissed his forehead, which made him smile. After that she pulled up a chair and sat down between them and said, "Young girls are always getting into difficulties." The girl didn't say anything. "Sometimes," Auntie Dolores went on, reaching to take the girl's hands, then holding them fast in her own, "it's good to get things off your chest."

part two

TRUE CONFESSIONS

1
Confession of Pride
Noreen—Age 12

Gladys, Noreen's nineteen-year-old stepsister, on her wedding day, trembling fingers applying lipstick—Cherry Berry Red—rubbing it off with a tissue, applying it again, catches a glimpse as Noreen moves like a shadow past the mirror.

"Don't hang around behind me like that," Gladys says. "You are making me crazy."

"Shut up." Noreen flops down on the edge of the big double bed they've shared for seven years.

She examines the cheap shiny shoes her mother bought her for this shitty wedding. At Payless. They have straps across the tops. They are shoes for babies.

"Look," says Gladys, "I'm moving out, but I'm not moving away. Gerry and me are going to be twenty minutes from here. By bus. You can visit us whenever you want."

"Sure," she sulks. "The happy couple. You and what's-his-face."

"I'm serious," says Gladys.

"Whatever." She quickly wipes away a tear that is escaping down her face. Then she gets off the bed, stands behind Gladys for a fraction of a second, and says, "You look like hell."

2
Confession of Lust
Noreen—Age 14

Her stepfather, Stupidhead Bob, stands in her way at the kitchen door, arm high up on the jamb, grinning at her, his belly hanging over his belt.

"So you think you're going out, do you?"

"That's right," she says.

"Going with that boyfriend, are you? The one with the tattoos?"

"That's right." She's hungry, but there's no way she's going to push past him into the kitchen. She hates the way he looks at her. Not that he's ever done anything. Nothing like that, anyway. He *looks*—that is his crime. She'd like to be that ancient Greek creature Medusa—the one with snakes for hair who could turn people into stone with a single look. She shoots him a look of her own, one that is poisonous and stony, so he won't dare look at her that way. But when she walks down the hall, she can feel his damned eyes on her body anyway—the whole time. She stumbles around trying to get on her shoes.

"What's your hurry? You goin' out dressed like that?"

"That's right," she says.

"You look like a hooker."

"Thanks." Go blind, you bastard.

"You'll be thanking me, all right, when your skinny little boyfriend helps himself to what you got advertised. And don't you whine, missy, and tell me he's not like that. All the males of the species are like that. They just need the opportunity."

"Everybody isn't like you, you know."

"Just don't go and get yourself knocked up," he says. "Like your mother."

"Asshole loser," she says under her breath, and tears out the door before he can say anything else. Anything being the fact that her mother, pregnant at seventeen "by some guy, he was just some guy, Noreen—I was young and stupid," and on welfare by eighteen, was finally "rescued" five years later by Bob. A story he loves to tell—like that's supposed to make her grateful or something.

Brad is waiting for her outside the convenience store where he has just gotten off work. He pulls her around the corner and opens his jacket and wraps her up inside it until she can feel his heat and his heart thumping against hers, and his slow kisses that make her knees go weak.

Later they will go to his house, because his parents are never at home, and she won't care if what they do sometimes feels good and sometimes doesn't. She will drown in his smell and sweat and saliva and the weight of him and how much he says he loves her

and how much he says he needs her. She won't care about anything else. Anything at all.

3
Confession of Sloth
Noreen—Age 15

Her mother, Grace, also known behind her back as Amazing,
folds her arms across her nubby purple sweater and demands,
"What's this?"

"This what?"

"Message on the machine. Here, listen for yourself." With a
long pale square-tipped fingernail, Amazing presses the play button, then stands back, drink in hand (cheap vodka disguised with
orange juice is the recent favorite), squinting through smoke from
a low-tar, low-nicotine cigarette.

It's Jolly Roger, the principal at her school. She hadn't counted
on him actually leaving a message on the answering machine.

She shrugs. "So what?"

"You've missed ten days this month. *Ten days!* And this is the
first I've heard of it."

"So throw me in jail."

Next thing, Amazing weaves over to the phone again and
squints at the dial. "I'm calling up your stepsister," she says, like
this is somehow a big threat.

Noreen rolls her eyes, drops into a chair, examines her own

nails, which need to be redone. Maybe this time she'll paint them each a different color just to piss everyone off.

"Yeah, Gladys," Amazing says, by way of a hello. Then yak, yak, yak, about how hard she works, how hard *Bob* works, how they can't turn their backs and "the kid" is always up to something. "I don't know what the hell she cares about." Her mouth is mushed to the phone. She looks over her shoulder, frowns at Noreen. "Okay. Yeah. Well, since you're such an expert I'll hand you over."

"Why aren't you at school?" Gladys says to Noreen.

"I dunno."

"Well, what do you do all day—while they're out?"

"I dunno. Sleep. Watch TV."

"Noreen, you have got to stop all this, you know. This goofing off. This dumb acting out."

"Why."

"Because. It isn't healthy."

"I don't care." Turning away so Amazing can't hear, she whispers brokenly, "Why should I?"

Gladys sighs, and after a long pause, says, "Baby girl, what are we going to do with you?"

4

Confession of Anger
Noreen—Age 16

When they were kids it was always Gladys who was there in the dark, whenever things were bad. Always Gladys who would move closer in their bed, sometimes holding her as the storms of their parents' relationship were going full blast outside their bedroom door. Always Gladys whispering, "I love you to the stars and back again. That's how much I love you. Don't forget, okay? Right up to the stars," all the while hugging her so tightly that she almost stopped breathing. It was always Gladys beside her if ever that door swung open. Then there her stepfather would be, outlined by the dim hall light, standing like a scary monster, just waiting for one more peep out of them, almost hoping for it, it seemed, so there could be hell to pay. And the first out-of-body experience she ever had happened during one of those times.

She was seven years old and she couldn't shut up. Something just possessed her. She was convulsed in nonstop giggles beside Gladys. Suddenly he was in the room. And then across it. He gave her this look. There was a sickening sharp pain in her arm as he lifted her in the air. Another part of her, she would later recollect, watched it all happen—looked down and watched Gladys cry and yell at him. After a million years he dropped her. She fell back on the bed. Silence.

"*Little shit*," he whispered finally, and left the room.

Her arm felt as if it were still up on the ceiling. Later though it began to hurt like it was being jabbed from the inside by sharp little poky things all trying to get out. She cried until Gladys left the room and came back with Amazing, who examined her and swore at Stupidhead—calling him a crazy bastard even though he wasn't there to hear her.

Gladys made her a sling out of green cloth. She wore it like a badge of honor for weeks, much longer than she needed to, and damned his eyes every time he looked at her. Even back then she was damning him to hell.

He didn't touch her after that. He picked on Gladys instead, until she escaped by getting married to Gerry.

Whenever she remembers how Stupidhead picked on Gladys, never giving her a moment's peace, always calling her a fat cow and a whore, and how she, Noreen, never once stuck up for her, she puts her pillow over her face in deep twisting shame and helpless anger.

Amazing and Stupidhead had a trashy-mouthed small dog named Ginger that they got a month after Noreen went to live with Gladys. It was taught to beg by barking, so the thing never shut up—especially on Sundays when she was forced to go and visit them.

Gerry would put his thick freckled arm around her. "Have a great time, kid," he'd say, with a big dumb smile. His eyes would go all watery. He couldn't stand Stupidhead.

"Stupidhead is *your* father," Noreen pleaded one time with Gladys. "Why don't you and Gerry come, too?"

"Because I don't like Stupidhead any more than you do. And I don't have to." Gladys looked at Gerry. He looked back, still smiling. Crazy about her like she was some kind of angel. Like he thought that he was good and she was good and together they were good beyond mere mortals. It was all so sweet that it could seriously give you diabetes.

"But they don't even like me," Noreen said accusingly, hoping that that would work and she wouldn't have to go.

"Listen, we have a deal, you and me." Gladys would now pull out her weird mental contortions about family loyalty. "They have to see you once a week, or you can't live with me and Gerry. It's only fair, Noreen. They are your parents, after all. When you turn seventeen you can do whatever you want about them. Okay? That's the rule. *Seventeen*," Gladys stressed. "So go on now. And please try to be pleasant, okay?"

"Even alcoholics deserve respect," Gerry added piously.

He had moved closer to Gladys, his arm now around her. As if they were already thinking about how, as soon as she was gone, they would breathe deep sighs and have a nice time together, finally free of this crazy person they were always stuck with.

Sometimes Noreen hates them both, and this feeling sits like a glowing hard lump of coal under her rib cage, right next to her jealous heart. She could show the exact burning spot to anybody who cared to ask. This is the worst anger of all. It's so bad sometimes, she thinks her heart will stop beating, and, if it does, it'll serve her right.

5

Confession of Covetousness
Noreen—Age 17

Wesley Cuthand. She has no clear memory of how he looked when they first met. She'd been stuck between Saskatoon and Winnipeg. Walking along the highway. Fed up with the last guy she'd hitched a ride with—an asshole who'd given her the creeps, she remembers that much. (When he'd stopped his car, just before Brandon, and got out to take a leak in the ditch, she'd jumped out and run across a field. "Hey! Come back here, you whore!" he'd shouted. She gave him the finger and kept on running. Ten minutes after she got up her nerve to walk along the highway again, this truck slid up beside her. She was still jumpy as hell from that last ride.)

On the other hand, Wesley has no such problems remembering details about how *she* looked on their first meeting. She had a backpack on her back and the skinniest little ass he'd ever seen. "The sun was almost down, except for a piece of the sky that was still on fire. That's how I remember it. Oh yeah, and the fields—and the hills off to the south—they were kind of blue and shadowy." That's exactly the way he says it—about the land and the shadows and how the sky was on fire, et cetera, et cetera. Sometimes he even starts there, goes on about her skinny little ass, and then, "I stopped the truck. You got in. Your eyes all big and pretty in your face."

"You said it was dark, Wesley. How could you see them?"

"I *did*! I saw them."

"Okay, go on."

He puts his hand over his heart. "I thought my breath would never come back." And gives a low chuckle.

"Go *on*."

"I'm not going to *hurry*, Noreen. *Relax*, this is a good story."

"*Tell* it."

Next comes the part where he offered her a stick of gum to calm her. She took it from him, eased it up to her mouth, never once taking her scared eyes from him. The first words either of them spoke (the truck still wasn't moving) came from Wesley, who said, laughing, "You look like a jackrabbit."

Apparently, she almost jumped out of her skin before asking, "Why?" After which she stared straight ahead.

The best part about hearing this story is feeling safe—lying on Wesley's bed, the sheets all tangled up and sour-smelling from not being washed in a while, his arm around her, her head against his chest while she listens to his voice rumble on through while he talks.

He recounts what he said next: "Why do you look like a jackrabbit?"

"Yeah. You think I look funny?"

"No. You're the most beautiful woman I've ever seen in my life." And he tells this part very seriously. Sometimes, odd as it seems, there are even tears in his eyes.

That's Wesley. He values the truth. The fact that he hardly ever gets it never stops him from expecting it.

So back at the truck, near Brandon, she said, "You are a weirdo," and yanked on the door handle.

"I'll drive you anywhere you want," said Wesley, and of course he meant it.

"Anywhere?"

"Absolutely anywhere."

"All right," said Noreen. "Drive me to Winnipeg."

"I was only going as far as Brandon," said Wesley. "And I'm almost out of gas."

"Then piss off," said Noreen, and again she started to get out of the truck.

"I'll drive you. I'll get more gas. What are you doing out here?"

"Walking," said Noreen. "And that's all you need to know."

They spent two days and three nights in a cheap motel on the outskirts of Winnipeg, with the moon outside their window at night, and at twilight the blue land that rolled flat out to the horizon. They stayed until Wesley's paycheck ran out and she suggested that he take her on home to where she lived with her brother-in-law, Gerry, and her stepsister, Gladys.

"You mean you live here? In Winnipeg?"

"Of course." She stood in the motel bathroom applying mascara, which, besides painting her fingernails in unusual colors, is the only makeup she ever wears.

"But I thought you were coming from Saskatoon."

"I hitched *to* Saskatoon," she explained, examining her teeth, rubbing a finger across them. "I hitched there with my boyfriend. It didn't work out. So I came back without him. That's where I was coming from. When you found me."

In his favorite story of their love, Wesley claims he knew right then and there that he was up to his neck beyond the point of no return. She was the most delicate beautiful thing he'd ever seen, he says. He was in love with her flax-colored eyes, her long silky hair, her small hands and feet, the way she'd curl up beside him like a kitten, the way she rode him at night till the stars seemed to shower out of the cosmos and fall all around them.

Gladys met them at the door as Noreen walked in with Wesley, and right away she started in. "Where the hell have you been? I've had the cops out looking for you and everything. We thought you were dead in a ditch somewhere."

"I went with Tyler. To Saskatoon," said Noreen. "Nice to see you, too."

"I'm *responsible* for you. You didn't even say you were going. Noreen, you've been gone for ten entire days! You're seventeen years old and you just keep screwing up. You're always screwing up. I can't stand it."

"I was going to quit my job anyway."

"You might have warned them. You'll never get a good reference now. I'm ready to give up on you."

"A reference for *what*? Working at a crappy burger place?"

Wesley shuffled around on the little green mat inside Gladys's door. He looked down at his feet, then at Noreen, then at Gladys.

"And who is this?" demanded Gladys.

"Wesley Cuthand," said Noreen, pushing past her. "He's my boyfriend."

"I thought Tyler was your boyfriend!" Gladys was practically shrieking.

"He's probably still in Saskatoon. He's a loser," Noreen called over her shoulder. She wasn't about to confess that by the time they'd hitched there, Tyler had run out of patience and kindness. In a hole called Bianca's Burritos and Burgers, he'd excused himself politely—that was Tyler all the way—stood, his straight brown hair falling all over his big-boned, wind-raw face, and gone off to find the washroom. He didn't come back. After about twenty-five minutes their waitress, who had eyes as big and dark as the craters of the moon, leaned over the table and said, "I think you should know something. Your boyfriend's gone, hon. All I know is he paid for your meal just before he went out the door."

Noreen tromped into her bedroom, found a big black garbage bag under a mound of dead clothes, and started stuffing things into it—whatever she thought she might need or miss, although she couldn't have cared less about most of it, quite frankly. She just figured it was the thing to do. She left her room with the bag over her shoulder.

"I'm moving out," she announced to Gladys.

"*What!*"

"I'm moving in with him."

Wesley smiled shyly at Gladys. "I'll take good care of her," he said.

"Where to? Noreen, don't you start rolling your eyes at me. Tell me where you are going to be at."

"Okay. Brandon."

"*Brandon?* Why Brandon?"

"Because. It's where he lives."

"So." Gladys folded her arms to calm herself and gather inner strength. It's what she always did, gather inner strength, Sweet Jesus (Gladys's expression), before she tried reason again.

If ever Noreen tried to think back to when things between Gladys and her got derailed, she found that she couldn't locate any actual moment. It had just been a gradual thing, until one day she realized that Gladys had stopped behaving like a real sister. Here she was, twenty-four years old, with permanent scowly lines between her eyebrows. She was getting to be a sour old woman before her time.

"Noreen," Gladys said finally, "when Gerry and me agreed to take you in, the deal was that you had to finish high school. *That* was the deal. And now just how are you planning to make a living?"

"Beats me," Noreen shot back.

She left without even saying goodbye, threw her bag into Wesley's truck, got in.

"Aren't you going to give her my phone number?" Wesley wasn't starting the truck, just sitting there in the driveway.

"Wesley," said Noreen, "I am a free woman. Now let's get the hell out of here."

But as they drove away she looked back, hoping to see Gladys at the window, or maybe Gladys standing out on her front steps waving, trying to get just one more glimpse of her baby stepsister, of the person she had once claimed to love to the stars and back again.

In Wesley's small apartment in Brandon, she stays at home all the time. Wesley goes to work at Dan's Construction. She starts her day with TV. She rolls over in bed and there's Wesley, his long black Cree hair tied back, jeans, T-shirt, boots, ready to leave for work.

"Which channel?" he asks, standing by the TV.

"Five," she says, or "two," or "sixteen." She doesn't care. It's six o'clock in the morning. Yet he wants to know and stays until she tells him.

Then he comes to her side of the bed, makes her sit up and put on a sweatshirt, and gives her a hug, and kisses the top of her head like she's a little kid. "Eat something," he says, and then leaves and doesn't get back for sometimes twelve or thirteen hours.

For the first couple of weeks, she feels that maybe he expects something from her besides sex. One day, when he comes home and asks her how her day went—and she has managed by that point to pull on a pair of jeans—she replies casually, "Oh, I was out looking for work."

He looks at her for a minute. Then he comes and sits down beside her on the couch. He doesn't put his arm around her like he usually does. In fact he looks really mad.

"What's wrong?" she says.

He doesn't answer. He gets up, goes into the bathroom, takes a shower. After that he's in the kitchen, where dishes have been piling up for about three days. He washes the dishes, puts them all away. Then he cooks hamburgers and pulls out some slaw and a bottle of cola from the fridge and brings them into the living room, where she is watching the same channel he turned the TV to before he left in the morning for work.

He sits silently and eats his burger, his dark eyes flicking back and forth between his plate and the TV. She starts to feel scared. She takes a couple of bites of her burger and can't eat any more. She wonders if she should say something. Then she starts to get pissed off. "What the hell is wrong with you?" she says. "I tell you I've been out looking for work and you go all weird on me."

He puts his hamburger very deliberately onto his plate. Brushes crumbs lightly from his hands. Thinks for a minute. Then he turns and says in a cold voice, "I don't care whether you look for work or not. That's up to you. What I don't like is when people lie to me."

"Lie to you? I don't know what you're talking about."

"Stop acting like a little kid, Noreen," he says, and goes back to eating his burger.

She tucks her legs tightly under her body and says to him, "Well, Wesley, I don't appreciate being treated like one."

"I don't treat you like a kid," he says, chewing away, staring hard at the TV.

"Yes, you do. You always do."

"When?" He's still staring at the TV. "Tell me when I do that."

"Every morning. You make me sit up like I'm some stupid invalid or something. And you make me tell you what channel. And then you make me put on a sweatshirt." She realizes even as she says this that she *is* sounding like a kid. But she goes on. "Maybe I don't want to get up, Wesley. And maybe I don't care about the stupid TV. Or my goddamn sweatshirt."

"Okay," he says. "I won't bother you anymore."

After that he leaves her alone. Every morning he doesn't wake her up—even though she is only pretending to still be asleep. He quietly rolls away until the mattress is light again with only her weight. He pulls on his jeans, makes coffee, pours himself a mug, and goes with it to the open window. He stands there with his bare brown back, making her feel jealous of the sun that he is saying good morning to. After he leaves she turns on the TV, pulls on one of his shirts, hugs it around her body, and then hates herself for missing him so much. Eventually she falls back asleep. When she wakes up again it's usually the middle of the day.

Things go along like that for a long time, her staying in bed most of the day, Wesley working right through into the evening. For a while she is too tired to care. She thinks she wants to go out and do something, then realizes she's been thinking the same thought for about an hour and hasn't moved from the spot where she is sitting or lying. In her spirit, she feels half dead. And lately, too, she's been feeling bloated and fluish.

"Something is very wrong with you," Wesley says to her one day. "Are you sick?"

She's just come from the shower and is sitting on the sofa with the towel in her hand and her hair dripping in long strings down her back. She doesn't answer him.

He takes the towel and wipes off her back. Then he uses it to dry her hair. He takes a long time. He loves her hair. "Maybe you should go and see a doctor," he says after a while.

"I'm not sick. I don't need to go to a doctor."

"Then let's go for a drive."

"Where?"

"Anywhere."

"Why?"

"Noreen," he says, placing the towel around her shoulders, "you need cheering up. You need something, that's for sure. You don't even want to leave this apartment anymore. And you've been acting more and more like a—depressed person. It's scaring me."

"What? Now you're telling me I'm crazy?"

His shoulders sag. He takes a deep breath, avoiding her gaze. "About a year ago I was in pretty bad shape. I ended up doing something real cowardly. And that—the thing I did—got all messed up in my head. I finally had to go see somebody about it. Even then it didn't help much." He leans forward, clasping his hands. Waits for her to say something.

"I can't believe you think I'm crazy! I am *fine*, Wesley! There is *nothing* wrong with me. Nothing. Nothing. Nothing. Can't you get it through your head? *I just want to be left alone.*"

But she really doesn't want to be left alone. That's the last thing she wants. She is just saying it to be miserable. One night, side by side on their backs in bed, she folds her arms tightly across her chest. She stares at the ceiling. His head slowly turns.

"Are you counting the stars?"

"What?"

"How many stars are up there?"

"Don't talk to me about stars."

"Take away the ceiling and there's millions, trillions, of stars," he says, ignoring her comment. "Out on the prairies on a clear night, you can see every one of them. As long as you can find the stars, Noreen, or even imagine them, you can convince yourself that you don't feel lonely."

A little breeze riffles through their open window. She lets her arms drop to her sides. She can smell his hair, his skin. Wesley always smells real good. She scoots over to him and throws herself across his chest. She holds on to him with all her strength. There is an empty feeling coming from him that scares her. It's like he's gone away somewhere and will never come back. She keeps holding on until, at last, his arms come around her. Then she falls into a restless dream-filled sleep.

She dreams of cars. Of standing along a highway as they all pass by. Every one of these cars contains a family. As they disappear down the long straight stretch of blacktop, she looks into their back windows and catches glimpses of children's faces and the odd bit of color that stands out—like the red sleeve of a sweater or the dark profile of a silky-eared dog. Sometimes white papers with brightly crayoned lines flutter out of the open windows and swoop freely across the landscape, catching against a fence, or tangling up with bushes.

In this dream the fathers drive the cars, are kind and patient with their children, and never raise a hand to them. And they all wear cowboy hats. She keeps waiting for one of these hats to blow away, too, but none of them ever do. Instead they vanish with the cars and the smiling dads.

The next morning Noreen wakes up and Wesley has already gone. She can't remember where she is for a moment and just lies there, smelling the morning smells coming in through the window. The air is fresh. It's the last day of June and the sun is shining. She turns her head to look out the window and the first thing she sees is the sky. It's so blue she feels as if she is floating up to meet it, becoming part of it. It is the bluest sky she has ever seen. She lies there for a while, gradually remembering that she has a body, that she's in a bed, that the bed is in Wesley's apartment.

When she gets up she's so full of energy she doesn't know what to do with it all. She finds an orange in the fridge, eats it. After that she makes coffee and, pretending she is Wesley, stands by the window, slowly sipping from his favorite mug.

She's dressed in jeans with nothing on top. She loves the way the morning breeze dances freely across her little pointy breasts. Somebody walks by on the sidewalk, a woman and her dog. For some reason the woman looks up. She does a double take and Noreen gives her a short manly wave, then goes back to examining the sky and drinking coffee, lifting it to her lips, putting her elbow way up to the side, just like Wesley.

She spends her whole day being him, and it feels great. She tucks one of his T-shirts into her jeans. She even pulls her hair back like him. Then she moves energetically around the apartment, cleaning it. She scrubs down the bathroom, takes out the garbage, washes all of their things, remakes the bed with fresh sheets. After that she still has energy. So she cleans the fridge, scrubs the stove inside and out, washes the floor. Next she starts on their tiny living room, which is also their bedroom, and dusts and tidies and sweeps.

By then the day has all but disappeared and she is hungry. There is nothing much to eat in the refrigerator. She considers making dinner, but there isn't anything very interesting in the cupboards either, so she goes on a search for money. She remembers that Wesley keeps spare change in a coffee tin on top of the kitchen cupboards. She stands on the counter, finds the tin, and brings it down. She takes off the plastic lid. There's change inside, all right, but also a lot of other money, mostly twenties. When she counts it all up, almost eight hundred dollars.

She takes one of the twenties and replaces the rest. Then she goes to Safeway, three blocks down at the end of the street. She buys a barbecued chicken, some potato salad and another kind of salad with corn in it because Wesley likes corn, two tins of iced tea, a small container of chocolate fudge ice cream, and a can of peaches. She struts back home. She's wearing an old pair of his boots, tied up tight so they'll stay on her feet. They make her feel tall.

At somebody's chain-link fence, a whole bunch of daisies have poked through the holes to freedom on the other side; she saw them on her way to the store. She sets down her bags of groceries to admire them, and picks some. She blows on them for luck. Then she picks up the groceries and walks back to the apartment.

When Wesley gets home from work, he sees the daisies on the coffee table. That's the first thing. Then he starts to notice the other things, how tidy stuff is, how clean. He goes into the bathroom and comes out again with a great big smile on his face.

"Are you hungry?" Noreen asks him shyly.

He responds with a chuckle that is pure Wesley, and says, "What—you're a cook, too?"

She walks proudly past him and takes their plates out of the fridge. She sliced everything up ahead of time, with a peach half for each, cut into the shape of a star. She hopes he'll notice this little detail. He does. He eats his peach half first, and smiles at her. She forks her dinner around on her plate. The combined smell of chicken and potato salad suddenly makes her feel ill. She picks away at her peach and waits for him to ask where she got the money to buy the groceries. Of course maybe he just thinks she still has some money left of her own. Besides, she only took twenty dollars.

Next morning she wakes up nauseated. She goes into the kitchen, discovers a box of saltines at the back of Wesley's cupboard, eats a dozen or so crackers, and immediately feels better. After that she stands up on the counter again, taking another twenty dollars out of the tin. She goes out in Wesley's boots and walks a little farther than the day before. She finds a Wal-Mart and once inside locates the sewing supplies. She looks through material—rows and rows of flat bolts. Nothing looks or feels exactly right. The salesgirl asks twice if she can help. No, says Noreen, I'm just looking—but she's beginning to feel discouraged. Then the salesgirl, whose name is Sylvia—it says so right on her tag—directs her to a round bin that contains tail ends of material, remnants on sale.

"Go crazy," Sylvia says, smiling, leaving Noreen to her own devices.

She begins by delicately pawing through the fabrics. Nothing. Then she starts hauling them out onto the long sales table, scattering the bright colors and textures everywhere. Three-quarters of the way through the bin, she finds what she is looking for, a big roll of gauzy dark blue with dime-size white blotches splashed randomly. She unravels a length, then stands back. When she half closes her eyes, she realizes, happily, that you could almost think it was the nighttime prairie sky. She pays Sylvia for the material, some needles and thread, and a cheap but workable pair of scissors with purple handles, and goes back to Wesley's.

At first she tries spreading the material out on the living-room floor, but that proves difficult because there isn't enough empty floor space. Then she remembers that it should be longer than the bed, so she measures it along the length and down over the end of the mattress. There is enough cloth to cut into two lengths, which she does, sitting on the floor. She sews them together up the middle and hems the ends. After the last stitch, snipping the navy blue thread with her teeth, she stands and flips out the cloth. The early afternoon breeze from the window puffs it up in the middle. Magically, the whole thing floats down on the bed, looking, she thinks—if you have a pretty good imagination—almost like a starry prairie sky.

One of the many TV shows she's watched over the past almost two and a half months since she's been living with Wesley showed a person covering a canopy frame over a bed. What she really wants is to put the sky over his head. She thinks of him at night, staring up, thinking his poetic thoughts. There is, however, no such frame on his bed. So she goes downstairs to the super to ask if she has a ladder and a staple gun. The super, Melissa, who is about fifty years old and always chews gum, has a ladder Noreen can borrow, but no staple gun.

Noreen takes the ladder, dragging it up five flights of stairs to the apartment. She sets it up by the bed, then goes into the kitchen and pulls down the can of money from the top of the cupboards. She takes out a twenty for the staple gun, rethinks this, and takes one more twenty—just in case it's an expensive item. She also has this idea that if she bought a couple of artist's brushes and a few pots of silver and gold paint, she could make points around some of those white spots and then they'd really look like stars. So she helps herself to another twenty.

At the end of the day, when she finally comes down from the ladder and looks up at the billowy blue material, all sparkly and celestial, she can't believe she has made this—made it just for Wesley. She lies down on the middle of the bed and looks up. Surely it's the nicest thing she's ever done for anybody. It certainly is the prettiest. She tucks her hands inside the waistband of her jeans. She's feeling bloated again and kind of ill. She undoes the button. Then the fly. Places her hands gently on her abdomen.

A dull memory, insistent as heat, creeps over her. She thinks back over the last couple of months. Tries to remember when she had her last period. Thinks about that time the condom broke when she and Wesley were going at it. And there were a couple of other times when they didn't bother with protection at all. Her mouth goes dry. Her whole being begins to shake with a terrible, sickening recognition.

Later, she doesn't hear Wesley come home. She doesn't hear his truck pull into the graveled side lot under their apartment window, or the tiniest dying rattle the engine always makes just as he turns the key and pulls it from the ignition. She doesn't hear him come into the apartment or close the door or set his boots down in the hall. She doesn't hear his feet on the carpet, or the familiar soft *clunk* his key chain makes when he places it on the coffee table.

She doesn't hear him standing there, breathing—looking at the expensive staple gun, the paints and the paint brushes, and her lying under the canopy of stars—or hear him going through the plastic bags to locate the sales slips, pull them out, and read them. She doesn't hear him as he stands thinking about all this, putting it together in his mind; or when he goes into the kitchen, pulls down the coffee can, pops the lid, takes out his money, and begins to count it.

What actually wakes her up is one, single explosive word: *"Shit!"*

Then he is standing over the bed, towering over it, over her. Just like a bad little monkey, she sits up and scoots over to the other side so he can't hit her, or grab her, or do whatever it is he's going to do to her.

"I'm missing a hundred dollars here, Noreen! Why the hell didn't you just ask!"

"I'm sorry. I'm sorry. I'm sorry," she says, putting her hands over her ears.

He looks up at the stars now sparkling dully from his ceiling and says again, *"Shit."* Then he turns abruptly, strides to the door, pulls on his boots.

"Please don't go."

"I need to get out of here. I need to think."

"Wesley, please please please don't go. I'll do whatever you want."

"And just what would that be?" he says coldly. "Get a grip, Noreen."

He slams out of the apartment. His boots make a terrible angry sound down the hallway, down and down the five flights of creaky wooden stairs, out of the building, onto the sidewalk. After that everything is quiet. She sits at the edge of the bed, thinking.

She thinks about her stepfather and how there was once a time when he was nice—before he married Amazing. "Just wait," Gladys had told her, the day after he gave her a Barbie doll she really wanted. "He's just doing that to impress everybody. You don't know him like I do. He's a crazy bastard." Gladys was right. He gradually changed into Stupidhead and didn't budge from there on.

She doesn't feel a single thing, she realizes now, shaking her head, and that's good. After all, she knew this was coming. Sooner or later Wesley would have grown tired of her and things would have changed. Taking his money without asking has just helped to speed things along. It's almost a relief this has happened. Now she can leave.

The purple-handled scissors she bought earlier are still lying on the floor. She picks them up and takes them into the bathroom. In front of the mirror, she solemnly regards the silky long blond hair that Wesley always loves to stroke. She lifts one section away from her head, moves the cool metal blades in until they are a few inches from her scalp, then snips. Instantly, a long snake of pale gold slithers into the sink. She does this with another section, and then another, until soon Wesley's sink is filled with her hair.

Then she takes the few belongings she arrived with, plus the money remaining in the coffee tin, coldly picks up his keys, locks him out of his own apartment, goes out and gets into his truck, and drives away.

part three

THE WAGES OF SIN

1

Even when the girl tried to pull away, Dolores had looked at her fiercely, making her look back, never once releasing her grip on those small fine-boned hands. In this manner the story had come out, its telling taking a very long time indeed.

All the while Lynda rushed back and forth trying to do everything herself. Later there wouldn't need to be any apologies from Dolores. They'd been friends long enough. Some things took priority over the odd too crispy pancake. So Dolores held on, delved deeper, made the girl go back and repeat herself whenever things needed clarification. Even as she was overcome by huge gulping sobs that shook her entire body, Dolores held on. That was how you loved somebody into telling the healing truth. And it felt good to be doing this. Dolores felt her old powers rise—something she hadn't felt since before Mirella got sick, when she could do nothing to help her own daughter.

After it was all out, Noreen whispered with raw shame, "I've done such bad things."

"Everybody's done bad things," Dolores shot back. "This doesn't excuse you now from trying to make things right. For instance, you could call up your stepsister and tell her how sorry you are for making her worry about you all the time. But first thing—look at me, Noreen—what you have to do *right now*, is get in touch with your boyfriend and tell him where you are."

"But I stole his *truck*!" Noreen wailed.

"So you've said."

"And his *money*! Nearly *seven hundred dollars*!"

"Yes. I understand."

"And I think I'm pregnant," Noreen sobbed. "It's his baby."

"This also is a form of stealing," agreed Dolores.

"I don't know what to do." She cried and cried. Then cried some more.

Dolores released her hands, gave her a napkin. "Do you love this boy?"

"No," said the girl, angrily wiping her eyes, blowing her nose. "I don't love anybody. Period."

She raised her eyes, which were now burning red and full of terror, and Dolores resisted an urge to reach over and hug her up good. This was the saddest little pumpkin she had seen in a very long time and, of course, she was remembering Mirella, bless her in eternal rest, who also had been full of woe all during her teenage years.

2

It would have been the easiest and best thing, Noreen thought, to just get the hell back in the truck and take off. But she couldn't think of where to go. In fact, she couldn't think at all.

The old lady in the pink sweatshirt had made some tea, set it in front of her, urged her to eat something and then had left her to go back out front and look after a couple of customers. It was around eleven-thirty. Hardly anybody was coming into the café now. The woman from last night, yawning over a cup of hot coffee, leaned against the stove and took a break.

The boy ran a tiny green tractor along the edge of the table until it bumped into her hand. Then he stopped, as if testing to see if this annoyed her. It did. But he kept on anyway, and she let him. He ran it up over the hills of her knuckles, to her wrist, along her forearm. He smelled like sunshine and dust and kid sweat and his breath was very sweet. The tractor reached her shoulder, sat there as he breathed and looked at her with solemn eyes and a funny little twist of his mouth.

"Noreen," he said at last, "are you sad?"

She didn't answer, but her heart also twisted just a little.

She waited twenty minutes, and then another twenty. Finally she felt brave enough to call Wesley. She got up and went to the phone and dialed his number. Four times it rang and then the answering machine kicked in. She was glad. That way she didn't have to talk to him directly.

"Wesley," she said. "It's me. It's Noreen. I took your truck. And your money. I drove south of Brandon in the rain, and I got lost, and I stayed overnight at some place called Pembina Lake. I'm not coming back to you, so don't even ask me to. If you want to call the cops that's up to you. And by the way I think I'm pregnant. If I am, it's yours, Wesley. No way it isn't. So don't pull any of that couldn't-be-mine shit on me. Anyway, I'm pissed off, if you really want to know the truth. This whole goddamn thing is a mess. And I am tired of my shitty life."

She had promised herself she wouldn't cry when she talked to him, but here she was crying to a stupid answering machine. She quickly put down the phone. Then she realized that she hadn't left a number for him to call back. But maybe she didn't want him to. She couldn't think what it was she actually did want. So she sank to the floor under the telephone and waited for some kind of idea to come.

The old lady came back and pulled up a chair, sat in it beside her, stared for a long time at the floor, and then said, "How long since you talked to your stepsister, Pumpkin?"

Noreen sniffed, wiped her eyes, examined the trail of smudged black mascara on the back of her hand. "Since I moved out for good. With Wesley. It's been over two months." She raised her eyes. "Are you Molly Thorvaldson?"

"I'm Dolores, remember?" She held out a handful of tissues and Noreen took them and blotted her eyes some more. "Lady you stayed with last night? That's Lynda. Café was named for her great-grandma, an Ojibwe woman who got hitched up with an Icelandic settler. So that was your boyfriend you just called?"

"I left a message."

Dolores nodded, then said slowly, "Your stepsister would also probably like to hear from you."

"Would you stop going on about her! I'm not calling. She doesn't want to hear from me. She's better off without me. We had a fight!"

"You can't stay mad at people forever. It ruins your sleep," Dolores pronounced. She then nodded many times as if what she had just said was a very big deal.

Noreen sighed. She had never met anybody quite like this—such a royal pain in the butt about the importance of her own opinions. She couldn't resist arguing with her. So she added hotly, "I'll bet you fight with lots of people."

Dolores looked her hard in the eyes. "Not lately." Then she rose and left.

The café gradually filled up again. The little boy, Seth, wandered off outside with the dog. Noreen sat in the kitchen by the window and looked out onto a tangle of uncut grass, hollyhocks, and yellow rosebushes. The smell of dog shit, mixed with the perfume of flowers, blew in on the hot breeze and made her gag. She went into the bathroom. It had blue wallpaper with pictures of waddling ducks—a border halfway up the wall. She threw up again. Flushed the toilet. Wet a bunch of paper towels with cold water, leaving the tap running, and held them to her face. She broke down crying once more, sobbed into the towels until they were hot with her tears, then got up, looked at herself in the mirror, and thought of that old cowboy expression, "This is the end of the trail, pardner."

3

Dolores knew that at five past the hour her friend Mary Reed would be coming through the door. You could always set the clock by Mary, and she certainly was in for an earful today. The clock above the counter now registered a little after four o'clock. The girl in the kitchen was sobbing hysterically. Her boyfriend's voice rose above the sobbing.

"That boy just came out of nowhere," said Dolores. "Sailed through the door like a storm cloud. Did you see him coming?"

"No, I certainly did not," Lynda replied angrily, "and I can hardly wait for them both to clear out. I can't believe I allowed her to stay in the first place. I must have had rocks in my head."

Lynda attempted to make more coffee that didn't need making. She spilled the grounds, slopped water all over the place. Dolores followed behind her with a wet rag, as she always did on days when Lynda was upset, and felt thankful there were no customers in the café.

Three minutes after four. Dolores pictured Mary limping into the town. Excitement from the previous night worn off—the new baby, Caitlin Louise, lived clear across the country in Prince Edward Island—she'd now be thinking: Who knows if I'll ever get to see this child? (Even though grandson Ronnie had recently offered his frequent flyer points.) *How ever did they think an old lady was going to navigate through all those big city airports?* That would be Mary. Scaredy cat.

Oh, well. Forget about it, Dolores thought. Nobody's perfect. Didn't I, for instance, leave her last night without saying goodbye? Yes, I did. And didn't I do it on purpose just to let her know how mad and upset I was? Yes, and that was very cold of me. And of course Mary, she'll have a beautiful pot roast bubbling away, just in case, in the slow cooker. Vegetables all around it. She'll be hoping for an extra guest at supper. That was Mary for you. First she drove you nuts with all her negativity. Then she'd do something real generous like the thing with the pot roast and you'd soften up—until the next time.

And here came Mary now, entering the cool of the old brick building, standing just inside the door, waiting for her eyes to adjust. Dolores watched her girlhood friend flatten her hair with a garden-roughened hand, remove a bobby pin and stiffly replace it, and tug on her blouse to make sure it wasn't riding up anywhere. She looked up just as Dolores rushed toward her.

Reaching out, Dolores grabbed Mary's plump arm, steering her to a back table where they both sat down.

"We've got trouble," whispered Dolores.

"So you say," sniffed Mary.

Then Dolores watched Mary's face. Its slow dawning. The awareness of the commotion in the kitchen. The yelling and screaming, a regular fight going on. Watched it stir her. Watched as she listened all the harder.

Passion had erupted in their little town, and that made her old friend very, very happy.

4

When Wesley strode into the kitchen of the Molly Thorvaldson Café, Noreen stood up out of sheer surprise. She felt a rush of relief. She wanted to leap into his arms, wrap her legs around his body, hold on to his neck, bury her face in his sweet-smelling hair, and never let him go again for as long as she lived. Then memory gripped her heart and sent her ass-over-teakettle onto the floor. Her legs were like rubber, all flipped out in front of her. She was stunned with fear and shame and the absolute certainty that the world as she knew it was about to come crashing to an end.

Wesley came over to her, stood clenching and unclenching his fists. "Did you think Pembina Lake wasn't on the map, Noreen?" His voice shook with emotion, a tornado hovering over the land. "I got a buddy to drive me and drop me off. Took us a little under an hour. And as for finding you here? That was easy. This town is about the same size as that picture I always keep of you in my wallet. Not to mention my truck being parked right out there in plain view."

"I'll give you back your money," Noreen said sickly. "I didn't spend any of the rest of it."

"I don't want my goddamn money!" he shouted. "I trusted you, Noreen. I loved you more than my own heart, and look at what you have gone and done to us."

She gave him back the money anyway—threw it at him. He shoved it into his pocket. Next thing he was asking for the keys to his truck. She was crying uncontrollably and couldn't see to get them out of her backpack. She shoved her hand down through all the useless trash of her life—gum wrappers, nail polish bottles, a pair of sunglasses, balled-up tissues, a ripped notebook, two pairs of underpants, her orange cotton bra—and finally connected with the soft smooth metal of his key chain. She hauled it out and threw that at him, too. It hit his leg and thunked down onto the floor. He bent over, swiped it up, turned to leave.

"Well, Wesley, I *never* loved you!" Noreen yelled at his back. "So good riddance. I hope you have a great life, you bastard."

He turned and came over again, sank down on his haunches, looked at her, his eyes all red and brimming with tears. "You are the hardest woman I have ever met," he managed at last.

Then, reaching into his pocket, he pulled out the money she had given back, carefully peeled off two hundred dollars, and handed it to her. Briefly laying one finger on her knee, he added, "If that baby you are carrying looks anything like me? I'll come back and give you my truck."

She could feel his breath on her face. If she let it, it would make a mark she would have to look at forever. It would bleed down her neck like a hot little arrow and come to rest in her heart. So she drew herself up until she stood over him. There, legs shaking, she replied, "Don't bother, Wesley. It'll never be born. I'll make sure of that."

5

Dolores Harper saw Wesley Cuthand leave the café and get into his truck. The little flame that had been growing slowly inside her all day made her leap out the door and go after him.

The window on the passenger's side was rolled down. As she laid her hands on the soft cream-colored vinyl, Wesley leaned dispiritedly over the steering wheel and started up the engine.

"I'm Dolores Harper," she said quietly, and extended her hand.

He looked up, startled, and noticed her for the first time. "Wesley . . ." he said, slowly reaching over.

"Yes, I know," said Dolores, as their hands met. "I heard the ruckus back inside."

Something in the clear-eyed way she looked at Wesley inspired his confidence. He blurted, "I feel like shit—if you'll pardon the expression," then sat back.

"You've got a nice truck here . . . almost brand-new and no dents that I can see," she said, deflecting his remark. "Maybe we should go someplace where you can simmer down." She raised her eyes to the deep blue sky. "It's a beautiful day." She lowered them again. "There's a place I like to go. Haven't been there since way back last fall. Seems like a long time ago now, that's for sure."

She stopped, then added for good measure, "It was cherry-picking time."

"Get in," he said, reaching to open the passenger's door.

The women in his family had all been bossy, from his great-grandmother right down through his five sisters. He had a lot of respect for strong-minded women and they never failed to cheer him up. Soon he and Dolores had rattled over the railway tracks and the tires were singing along the highway that led out of town.

"See that bump over there?" She directed his attention to Tiger Lily hill, the highest point in the valley's west-facing escarpment. "It's about ten minutes from here. The turnoff's coming up on your left. We'll go over there and sit, and have a good look at the valley. You can see it all from up there."

She folded her arms across her chest. It was nice to be driving along with a handsome young man. She could understand why girls might like him. His long crow-colored hair. He smelled real good, too. It reminded her of when she was young and met Raymond and how he first courted her by offering his hand to dance a jig up at Pine Bluff. Back then, he was as debonair as a movie star. Ah, Raymond, with his muscular arms. Raymond, with his hands on her body. The babies they made together, then lost through miscarriage—each loss drawing a deeper silence between them in their bed. And then the day he held Mirella, like a miracle, for the first time. "She ain't pretty," he said with an ear-to-ear smile, "but she's cute enough. Guess we won't send her back."

They arrived at the high plateau. Wesley pulled the truck onto a rutted dirt trail lined with chokecherry bushes, the berries still a bitter green but already beginning to droop from their stems. A No Smoking sign dangling from his rearview mirror swung back and forth to the rhythm of the rough ride. Soon the trail petered out. Dolores directed him over unbroken land for three or four more minutes until they came to where they could see a big stretch of the valley, with its sloughs and slow-moving creeks and Pembina Lake spreading off to the south. Wesley turned off the engine. They sat for a while, not talking, the windows rolled down, the hot sage-smelling wind blowing off the land and filling up the truck with the kind of peace and quiet you only get when you forsake the well-traveled spaces.

"Good deep spirit here," Dolores said, breaking the silence. "I know a man who drives up to this exact spot every Sunday morning. I go to church myself, but keep close company with Mother Earth—what my friend Lynda refers to as the Goddess or the Whole Enchilada. Whatever calls a person is okay by me. I figure we're all connected." She settled farther back into the cream-colored seat. "Do you believe in something, Wesley?"

"I believe in work," said Wesley, looking out disconsolately at the valley.

Dolores chuckled. "That's a modern malady."

"Been working since I was eleven years old. Started out delivering flyers. After that I helped my uncle haul gravel. Then I learned how to drive big machines. It pays the bills." He smiled feebly. "Bought me this nice truck you're sitting in."

Dolores sat very still, pulling in her knowledge of him from what Noreen had told her. She would lead him through a series of statements to the heart of the matter. It would be a delicate ride. "You're very young," she said, warming up.

"Almost twenty-one. Birthday's at the end of August."

"Sometimes it's good to stop rushing around and take time to think about things," she countered to surprise him.

It worked. He looked at her, startled, then said shyly, "I do that all the time. Company I work for gets contracts just outside the city. On my lunch break sometimes, I slip away by myself. Disappear for maybe a half hour or so."

Dolores nodded her approval. "Maybe then you're the kind of person—just like my husband, Raymond, rest his soul—who can sit on the side of a prairie bluff and see answers in the heat waves rising off the land."

"Never gotten that far."

"I also know a man who can turn his troubles into poetry," she said, adding cautiously, "It's a real gift."

"I've never written a poem in my life."

Dolores closed her eyes as if she were divining. This was too easy. The young man was a pussycat. "And how did you meet your girlfriend?"

So Wesley found himself spilling out his favorite story, omitting a few of the more flamey details because those parts were nobody's business. Of course he also left out the part about how screwed up in his head he'd been until he found her, like an answer to his prayers. Next he moved on to their life together in his cramped apartment, telling about how he took care of her and gave her all his love but Noreen was so messed up he didn't think she would ever be happy.

"Being happy isn't everything," said Dolores. "You only sleep good when you are being a good person."

Wesley had to think for a minute—because she'd stopped him in midstory—before he replied softly, "I was pretty much the best person I could be when I was with Noreen. She makes me happy. *Made* me happy."

Dolores reached over and took his soft girl-shaped hand in hers, marveling that this hand drove heavy-duty machinery. "It seems to me," she said, "that you have responsibilities now."

"It might not be my baby," he protested. "She's had other boyfriends. Besides, she doesn't want me. She said so. She just likes breaking people's hearts," he added bitterly.

She thought about this, then continued kindly, "As things stand at this very moment, Wesley, *somebody* is going to be a daddy."

He sighed a deeply troubled sigh, didn't remove his hand from hers, and she watched his eyes fill up with tears. She gripped his hand more firmly than ever. Poor boy, she thought, your heart-ache is only just beginning.

6

When Dolores got back, Mary Reed was still cooling her heels at the café. Mary looked up, saw Dolores, frowned, then said pointedly to Lynda, who was refilling her mug with coffee, "Why doesn't somebody sit down for a change?"

Something about the angle at which Mary was sitting—her hands stiffly arranged around the white mug—pulled Dolores back to last fall. That last berry-picking expedition. Mary had not been herself. She had looked tired. They'd had an argument about something. For the life of her, Dolores could not now recall what that argument had been about. But when she saw her friend again a couple of days later, Mary had seemed even more tired. Dolores remembered saying, "We don't have to make the jelly today." But Mary had raised a hand, the flesh puffing out around the gold rings on her fingers, and said, "Let's get it done." That had been right around the time she'd stopped driving her car—stopped going out much at all as a matter of fact. Well, she would have to ask her about this later.

Lynda was already making her way back to the kitchen. "Got coleslaw to make. There'll be a few stragglers for supper and then I'm finished. I'm closing up early today. It's been a strange week."

"Sorry I was gone so long. I'll help," Dolores assured her. "I'm sure there's cleanup to do. You stay where you are, Mary. Just sit and drink your coffee."

But Mary picked up her cup, rose stiffly, and followed them. "You need to hire somebody, Lynda, full time," she said.

"I simply can't afford to do that," said Lynda.

"Of course you can. Stay open longer hours. Attract more business."

"I have a son to think about."

Dolores thought, Keep quiet, Mary, can't you see she's had enough for one day? But Mary, as usual, opened her big mouth and kept right on. "You are always closed on Sundays. And Mondays. Who ever heard of such a thing!"

Lynda groaned. "There's just not enough business. And besides, then I'd always be open. I can hardly stand it as it is. I'd sell this place in a minute, except nobody would buy it. I'm just trapped."

"Trapped," said Mary indignantly, her face coloring with anger. She lifted one shoulder like a prizefighter about to make a move, set her jaw, and let her pronouncement fly. "You're going to get old and nasty like me and they'll bury you up there on cemetery hill, right between your mother and Joe Hartman—with scraggly lilac bushes every single summer and ass-high snowdrifts for an eternity of winters. Now that, my girl, is trapped."

Well, now the damage is really done, Dolores thought. She watched Lynda's whole body droop with defeat.

Then Seth, standing in the middle of the kitchen, demanded that Lynda make him a sandwich, on *white* bread, spread with *brown* sugar, heated in the microwave.

"In a minute, baby," said Lynda with the look on her face that she wore more and more frequently—as if she was moving through her life in a thick fog. A sure sign, Dolores thought, of what old-time people would call "spirit sickness."

"I'm hungry," Seth whined.

"I'll make it for you," said Mary. "But only if you'll say please. And go wash those hands. You look like you've been out digging in the garden."

Seth said please, roared off to the bathroom, flipped on the tap, splashed water around in the sink, then wiped his still-grimy hands on his mother's pale blue towels. The girl, Noreen, had been in there again and she had left an empty box on the top of the toilet tank. He brought it out to show Auntie Dolores and Auntie Mary and his mom.

Upstairs, on the cot with the pink quilt, Noreen lay on her back and contemplated her ruined life. Wesley was gone. She was pregnant for sure—that stupid test had just said so. There was no way she would swallow her pride and call Gladys. Stuffed in the side pocket of her backpack was the money he'd handed back. At least he'd thought that much of her. At least he hadn't left her completely stranded, like her last boyfriend. Well, she *would* get an abortion. Then she'd get a job somewhere, anywhere, and try not to dwell on the past.

As soon as she had those thoughts though, she had one other: *Who will love me?* Instantly her heart turned cold with dread. She fell asleep and dreamed she was out on the highway again, hitching. Only there were no kind cowboy fathers driving big cars filled with children and dogs. This dream was filled with blood and knives and men who wanted to hurt her. She found a cardboard box lying in a ditch, climbed inside, and hid there, trembling.

7

Lynda went out the back door with a bag of garbage and found the dog lying on her side, groaning. She also found evidence everywhere in the grass that she'd been sick. A foul stench rose up around her and Lynda's first thought was that she'd been poisoned.

"Tessie," she murmured, stroking the broad head.

The dog kicked her back legs in a kind of spasm. Lynda knelt to lift Tessie and staggered under the seventy-five-pound deadweight over to her little red hatchback. She laid the dog down, opened the car door, and then, picking her up again, struggled and pushed until she was stretched out on the backseat.

She went back inside where Seth, at the table, innocently tucked into his second slice of microwaved bread with brown sugar.

"Tessie's ill," she said quietly to the others.

Dolores turned, wiping her hands on a towel. Mary looked up from sweeping bread crumbs off the counter.

Seth put down his snack. "I *told* you something's wrong with her. This *morning*. But you didn't listen."

He got down from the table and started running for the door. But Lynda caught him, hunkered down to his level, held both of his hands in hers, looked steadily into his eyes. "You have to stay here, sweetie."

"What's happened to my dog?"

He was very close to tears. She wondered how much she should tell him. "I think Tessie may have eaten something that made her sick. So I have to take her to get some medicine. Okay?" She stood up quickly and Dolores and Mary drew close, circling Seth. "What about our little mother-to-be upstairs?"

"We'll *all* go to my place," Mary assured her. "Got a pot roast cooking back at the house that'll be as dry as a cat by now. But there's enough for everybody. Come on by when you've finished up at the vet's."

"Go on now," said Dolores. "We'll take care of closing up. I'll do the cash."

Upstairs on the bed, heart pounding, Noreen fell from the fuzzy world at the edge of her dreams.

"Noreen," a voice was saying, "my dog is sick."

She opened her eyes. Tried to focus. Failed.

"Tessie is sick," the boy pressed—rattling her, shaking her. "Wake up, Noreen. Okay?"

"What?" Just please, please disappear, she thought.

But he wouldn't. "My dog," he continued, "ate something bad and now she's sick."

A vague picture grew. Last night. Lightning flashes brightening Lynda's living room. Looking for the TV remote. Finding something gross instead—a slimy bone—and throwing it at Tessie.

Noreen came fully and irritably awake. All remnants of sleep had shuffled the hell off. "I gave her something last night," she told him, rubbing her eyes. "It was gross. But she wanted it. She'll throw it up. Dogs always upchuck stuff. Now go away."

"We don't give her stuff just 'cause she wants it," Seth persisted solemnly. "Some dogs want chocolate. But you don't give them chocolate. Chocolate poisons dogs. Did you give her chocolate?"

"You can leave now." Noreen smacked at her pillow, rolled over, and gave him her back.

"We have to go."

"What?" she said, annoyed, to the wall.

"We have to go with Auntie Dolores and Auntie Mary. Mom's gone to the vet's. Noreen?"

She was still facing the wall. She wasn't moving. A very bad feeling had begun to grow inside her. "What is it?" she said at last.

"What *did* you give my dog?"

8

Delbert Armstrong, fresh lumber for the addition to the main deck bouncing in the back of his truck, returned from his errands in the city. He dug into his jeans and pulled out his pocket watch, flipping open the gold casing to check the time.

He was thinking about the quiet inside Danny's cottage. Used to be he'd hole up there after Danny died—winter evenings, another log on the fire, a glass of whiskey in one hand, the family photo album in the other. He'd drink steadily until the photos blurred. Reaching drunkenly over, he'd pick up old birthday cards or yellowed newspaper clippings that had fluttered out from their hiding places between the dark pages of glued-in family moments. Maybe a card to their mother, "Happy Mother's Day, Mum—from Dan and Del." Nobody in the family had ever signed with love. Maybe a picture of himself at seven, holding up a silver pickerel as long as his arm, mugging for the cameraman, who was Danny. Then there were the later photos of him and Danny building the cottage together. In one, the best one, they are shingling the roof, shirtless, waving down from the sky like a couple of gods at Vera, Danny's fiancée.

Now so much time had passed. After Danny drowned, Vera moved to Calgary. Thirty-five years was a long time. And yet there was the odd day—especially now that he was sober—when he remembered what it felt like to be seventeen again.

He had just rolled on through Willow Point when, on the south side of town at the little vet clinic on the Mouse River, he noticed a familiar red hatchback parked out front. His heart danced a couple of beats. He slowed right down to a halt, there at the side of the road out of everyone's way. He figured something must be wrong with that dog of theirs. Maybe he should go and see if he could do anything to help. He sat in the lonely cab of his truck deliberating for several minutes, wondering how it would look, him just showing up like this.

"The hell with it," he muttered, and then circled back.

He discovered Lynda in the waiting area. She was the only one there, it being long past suppertime. Her head was bowed, she looked tired; that marvelous red-gold hair spilled over her face. He was torn between sympathy and rapture.

"Lynda," he said, going over to her. "Just passing by. Saw your car."

She lifted her head. She'd been crying. "Hi," she breathed. She pulled a tissue out of her jeans pocket and blew her nose. "Tessie's sick," she said. "It looks pretty bad. They're taking X rays . . ." Her voice caught.

He removed his hat, a gesture of respect for her predicament, and smoothed his hand over his wild hair. "I'll stay," he said. "Until you find out."

"You don't have to do that," she said, sniffing, blowing her nose again.

"Yes, I believe I do."

Lynda stared at Del. After such an awful day, she was so grateful for his company that she started to cry again. It was embarrassing. But it was also okay. In the end it was quite all right to sit wordlessly with this bashful man in the waiting area, surrounded by posters of dogs and cats, warnings about heartworm, exhortations to vaccinate your pet regularly, smells of fur and fear and medicinals, and the window that faced west with the northern sun still hanging over the evening hills. And when, half an hour later, the vet told Lynda she could come and look at the X rays, it seemed natural that Del would stand up, too, and follow them to hear the news.

Dr. Marina Howard, a harried woman with tired eyes, directed their attention to an image of Tessie's intestines. "What's she been eating? This looks like splintered bone. See, here—this arrow-shaped shard? It's lodged inside her guts." She looked accusingly at Lynda. "Chicken is the usual culprit."

"I've never given her anything like that," Lynda said, her heart suddenly pounding. "I would *never* give her chicken bones."

"Right," said the vet, as if she didn't believe a word of it.

"I'm very careful. I honestly am . . . although . . ." She paused, then continued, "I have to confess I *do* remember my little boy was eating chicken . . . but he would never . . . I mean I've taught him . . ." Her voice trailed away.

"Sometimes children unwittingly feed animals things they shouldn't," said the vet, slightly softening. "Was there, by any chance, projectile diarrhea?"

Lynda watched Dr. Howard's lips move, processed the words, and then managed, "I . . . I didn't notice. I guess I should have. I found her, you see, after she'd been sick. Quite a while later. She was lying down . . ."

"I'll give her something to calm those spasms in her guts, and some antibiotics. We'll need to keep her here."

"Here?"

The vet stared evenly at her. "Tessie may need surgery. But there is a chance that the bone might work its way through. It's a waiting game at present. You go on home now. You can come back in the morning and visit her if you like. We're open at eight."

When they got outside to the parking lot, Del surprised her. "Leave your car. I'll bring you back in the morning."

His offer was painfully sincere. He stood with the lowering sun at his back, slightly hunched, awkward, as if he expected nothing.

"Okay," she said uncertainly. But on their way back to town she admitted gently, "I'm awfully glad for this ride. I was just about at my rope's end. Thanks, Del."

"Don't mention it," he said, blinking at the road ahead.

Twenty minutes later they were back at Pembina Lake, parked in front of Mary's little bungalow with its spectacular view of the lake. The intimate light of evening was slowly descending, and Lynda found herself telling Del about Noreen.

While she talked, Del avoided her eyes, looking over instead at Mary's kitchen window, which was all lit up. She always left her Christmas lights hanging there year-round in an optimistic display of shabby merriment. "No bus comes through here until next Friday," he said a few minutes later.

"I know that," Lynda said. "With any luck at all she'll decide to hitchhike."

"Maybe she should stay for a while." He wiggled his thumb at the cottages along the beach below. "Maybe she could use Danny's place down there."

"Don't even think about it!" Lynda said, shocked. "You've spent a small fortune on it—building on to what was already there. We've all been waiting for you to move in."

He looked sharply at her.

"I'm sorry. I thought that's what you were planning to do. Dolores told me that now you've even winterized it."

74

He slapped some dust off his knee. "Cottages are for families, Lynda . . ." He stopped, nodded his head, gripped the steering wheel of his dead-still truck.

Lynda was stricken by this. She tried to think of something else to say. Everything she thought of would be wrong. Then she thought about how she'd known Del for years—about how in a small town you knew everybody for years. But people always kept something back. It was how you survived the close scrutiny of living elbow to elbow—the feeling of always being on display. It also kept people lonely, with private heartaches they never dared to talk about. Like Joe Hartman. On the day her mother was buried, he had put his arm around her shoulder and then held her close and kissed her cheek three times. She was twenty-three years old. In all the years she'd known him he had never done anything like that. Had never touched her in affection. But in that moment she realized she'd never given him the chance for what he'd wanted all along—to be a father to her.

Del would have been about the same age then as she was now. Back in that time he drank and roared around and had a horrible reputation with women. Now here he was sitting beside her—shy and sober. She looked at his profile, the still-lean line of it. They were strangers in this little ship of a town. Is that the way it would always be?

Del leaned against the window and said in a low voice, "Looks like Mary's expecting you. Let's go inside now. You can introduce me to the girl."

9

Noreen listlessly helped Seth draw a picture on a long sheet of white paper. An ice-cream pail full of broken crayons had been dragged out from under Mary Reed's musty stairwell. Some of the crayons were so ancient that they had grease spots on their wrappers. Still, they made good colors on the page. The smell of wax eased the feelings of despair that had been gnawing at her all day.

"I like yellow," said Seth. "Do you like yellow, Noreen?"

"It's okay."

He climbed onto her lap so he could reach their picture on the kitchen table, spread out before them with its brilliant meadow of green grass, yellow flowers, and blue sky. She wished he would just go away. Only a couple of hours ago he'd been so upset about his dog that he'd stomped down the road ahead of everybody and Dolores had asked him to slow down because of cars. When the other old lady made a grab for his hand, he'd shouted, "No!" as he ran ahead. Now that he seemed to have forgotten about the dog, he was back to being a pest. Even as she sank lower in the seat, he held on by wrapping his short skinny legs around hers and digging his sticky toes into the backs of her calves.

Both the old ladies were preparing dinner, all the while spying on Lynda Bradley, who apparently was parked outside with somebody. At the sink Mary tossed a handful of chopped apple and cabbage into a bowl and stared past the depressing string of dusty lights around her kitchen window. "He's still there. And she's not budging. Well, we'll find out soon enough."

Dolores walked over, threw a spoon in the sink, and said, "She could do worse."

"What are you talking about?"

"Them."

"Lynda and *Delbert*? Dolores, the heat's getting to you. What could our Lynda possibly find of interest in Delbert Armstrong, of all people."

Dolores shrugged. "There's no accounting for passion. And besides, he has a real artistic spirit."

Noreen put down a yellow crayon, searched for a blue one. Suddenly Seth squirmed off her lap, slithered under the table, and came out running on the other side.

"Del!" he shrieked.

Mary called after him, "Don't bang—!"

The screen door whined on its hinges, then slammed shut.

A few minutes of silence. Noreen finished the sky, began a flock of red birds. She was thinking about passion. About what the word meant. She supposed that what she felt for Wesley was something like passion. At first, of course, it had been a convenience. He was there. She was desperate. Later, though, it had turned into heat—rising up her legs, spreading heavily through her body, so that even her blood felt thick and slow. What she felt for Wesley also made her feel sick with longing. Was that passion, too?

She tried to think about what she had felt for her other

boyfriends. She realized that they had all made her feel lonely. She still felt lonely. Except when she had been with Wesley that had started to change. Sometimes in the morning when she rolled over he'd be looking at her. It was several weeks before she realized he enjoyed watching her sleep. And sometimes for just a moment or two, with Wesley watching her, his dark brown eyes pooled with light, she felt like she did when she was a little girl, safe with Gladys, being told she was loved to the stars and back. That wasn't passion. It was something else. But what? Her stomach knotted again. She felt drawn and empty.

Noreen brushed a hand across her face. Dug her fingers into her hair. Thinking, thinking, thinking. She hated thinking—it made memories press up against you like little demons with hot hot breath. She wouldn't think. Instead she picked up a cobalt blue crayon, bit into it. She hadn't done this since she was about seven years old. The taste of crayons used to make her feel better. Except not today. Her mouth immediately filled with oily wax; the scent pushed back up through her nostrils and sickened her. She spit the crayon into her hand, looked at it, all crumbled and wet, and smeared the whole mess on the underside of Mary's table.

Seth reappeared with Lynda and a very tall older man who wore a cowboy hat. He took off the hat, ran his hand through a field of thick graying hair, and nodded to her. No smile. She nodded back and couldn't take her eyes away from him. It was like he'd stepped out of those dreams she'd been having about cowboy fathers. She wondered if this was some kind of omen. Probably, with her luck, it was a bad one. Maybe the dog was dead. Or at the very least deathly ill.

They were introduced. She watched as Del sat down across from her, politely taking in his surroundings. Mary brought him a cup of coffee and said slyly, "Nice of you to give Lynda a ride over here, Del."

Lynda disappeared to another part of the house. Dolores quickly followed her. Seth, pushing himself under Del's arm until he was held in a kind of hug, looked up at him, and said uncertainly, "Is my mom mad at me?"

"Nope."

"And what's happened with Tessie?" Mary asked Del.

"Dog has a problem with her guts."

"Delbert Armstrong," Mary said irritably, "you are the soul of information!" She wiped her hands on a towel and went to locate Lynda and Dolores.

Noreen swept the drawing with the heel of her hand, smearing the red birds.

"I'm going with you tomorrow," said Seth. He banged his head against Del's chest, chanting, "I need. To see. My dog."

"Watch that now," said Del with an explosive laugh. "Don't strain yourself."

Seth flipped around until he was dangling backward off Del's knee. He was rescued—and now they were both laughing—as he slowly slid toward the floor.

Noreen drew more flying birds, strangely jealous of Del and Seth. Of their apparent closeness. She let that jealousy seep inside her. Gradually fill her up. It was better than being weakened by anxiety and sadness. She would hold on to it like a precious thing. She put down the red crayon. Selected one that was dark puke green. She used it to color beneath the blades of grass at the bottom of the page, working at their roots so that the jewel green meadow now floated on a shadow that was as long and murky as a crocodile.

But later out on Mary's deck—the citronella candles gleaming, the stars entering the immense stage of the sky, a sliver of moon hanging over the dark lake, and Seth squeezed in beside her on a wide wooden chair—something sweet started to trickle down inside her, catching her off guard.

Around midnight people began collecting their things, purses, jackets, sweaters. Seth was asleep against her. Lynda woke him and pulled his warm body away. He staggered sleepily to his feet. Noreen realized that she didn't want any of them to go. She was filled with panic about what would happen next. What she would do. Where she would go.

Delbert Armstrong, hat perched on the back of his head, came over to where she stood, feeling smaller and smaller, hands in her pockets, bare feet growing cold on the rough wood of Mary's deck.

"Got a cottage I'm not using," he said solemnly. "You'd be welcome to stay there."

10

Lynda sat outside in the truck with Seth, waiting while Del took Noreen in, showed her around, gave her the keys. She felt uneasy about the whole thing. The cottage, a handsome cedar structure, had sat pretty much unused for years. And now the addition—its fresh wood smell—that Del had built on his own over the past couple of summers. She couldn't imagine why he would offer to set Noreen up here.

Last spring when she'd discovered that Seth had stolen Del's watch, she'd been mortified. They'd immediately driven out to his farm just north of town, where Seth tearfully confessed and apologized. Del took back the watch in his gritty hand, the newly cultivated prairie fields stretching behind him. He didn't look angry or happy or even surprised. All those weeks he'd come into the café, asking if anything had been turned in, and yet here he was acting like a man who'd just picked up a stone and absently stuck it in his pocket. He then invited Seth, with her permission, to sit up in the cab of a big green John Deere tractor. She watched as they took half a dozen lazy turns around the field. By the time they got back they were buddies. "Well, what do you know about that," said Del as they walked over to her. "We've made your mother smile."

The light over the door of the cottage came on. A couple of seconds later Del himself appeared.

"You're sure it's okay for her to stay here?" Lynda asked.

"Yup." He started up the truck.

Then he drove them home, where she thanked him for everything he'd done that day. He looked uncomfortable with her gratitude, and brushed it off, saying he'd be back around eight the next morning to take her and Seth over to the vet clinic and check in on Tessie.

Lynda carried Seth inside and got him to bed. She decided not to ask if he knew anything about the bone Tessie had swallowed. It would just upset him. Now he wanted to say a prayer to the Universe and Jesus and the Goddess and the Creator for all the good things that had happened that day. He asked that Tessie get better and come home soon. She looked down at his pink face as he said his prayer and felt guilty about his peculiar religious education, about this life they were living, and about the loneliness she was subjecting him to.

Then she kissed him and held him and remembered the morning she'd found the courage to leave her husband, Larry. How scared she was driving out of Winnipeg in the middle of that bitter February blizzard, ice pellets bouncing off the windows, car heater moaning. And Seth sitting beside her, buckled up in his car seat, bundled in his scarf and snowsuit and that blue toque that kept falling off his head, his hair standing up from the electric dryness of the cold, his face as solemn and tearless as a little old man's. How she drove and drove and kept on driving until they found their way back to the only place in the world where she knew there were people who still remembered her.

Wesley Cuthand sat in his truck outside the apartment he and Noreen had shared and missed everybody. He missed his mother. Never mind that she was a constant nag who had always been on his case and had never given him a moment's peace the entire eighteen years he'd lived at home. She was the best mother alive. He missed his five sisters—every one of them smarter than he was and inveterate nags on his behalf as well. They were the best sisters alive. Everybody was spread right across the country. How was it that you could be crazy about the people in your family and then you never got to see them? Other people had families they couldn't deal with, or just plain hated, and they got to see their relatives all the time. What kind of perverse twist of fate was that?

For two cents he'd go back to Saskatchewan. Nothing had turned out right since he'd come to Manitoba. Two months after the move he'd found his first girlfriend here, Chantelle. He was happy. He had a good job and a great girlfriend. Well, great at first, until he found out she'd been screwing around on him with just about every guy in his construction crew—except, of course, for his friend Martin, who just might have been lying, and Mitch, the foreman, who was a sixty-three-year-old grandfather with prostate problems.

After Chantelle he got this feeling that was just a generalized sadness at first, but then it grew like a monster. It prowled around inside his soul. He was beginning to recognize that maybe he had bad luck with women. There had been Jackie, his girlfriend of over a year and a half, who, face it, had dumped him for a bodybuilder and had been the reason he left Saskatchewan in the first place. Lonely and angry, he kept right on working—taking longer shifts whenever they were offered. He mostly kept to himself.

One evening as the sun was going down, he was driving blind, so much inside his own head that he didn't notice a dog as it leaped up from the ditch onto the road—a blur of brown fur—and thunked with sickening finality under the wheels of his truck. It was still quivering when he turned, went back, and got out, sinking down beside it, lifting its head onto his leg. The tongue lolled. The staring eyes were glazed with road dust. Finally the dog became very still. It was somebody's pet—it said "Rex" right on the collar—there was even the owner's name and phone number. But now it was dead and he had killed it. Something came loose inside him. He got back in the truck and howled with grief all the way back to his apartment. For a few weeks he could not get over the guilt of never having phoned the owner. Of just leaving the animal there, its spirit hovering in a lonely space on that stretch of road. This feeling grew. When the animal began to follow him into his dreams every night, he decided to talk about it to a shrink, who assured him, "You're not going crazy. You just attract the wrong people and then they let you down and you blame yourself. Maybe what you need is a vacation."

What a dead-end life. He wanted more. Instead he'd fallen for another girl who had broken his heart, who had stolen the money he had, by working overtime, been carefully slipping aside for something special, like maybe even an engagement ring if things had worked out for a change.

Worse still, now they were split up and she was going to have a baby and he was such a coward that he couldn't deal with the fact that he could well be the father. In the first couple of weeks after he'd found Noreen hitchhiking on that same stretch of road where he'd killed the dog, they were both so careless that it could easily have happened.

He got out of his truck, let himself back into his place, pulled off his boots, lay on his cold bed, and looked up at the crazy starry sky Noreen had erected on the ceiling. He got off the bed, stood up, and felt like an old man. He went into the bathroom. Looked over and noticed Noreen's pale hair which, only hours before, he had discovered in the sink and thrown into the wastebasket. Thought about the sweet silky weight of it. Stood by the sink, leaning against it, hands now beginning to tremble. Looked at his reflection in the mirror.

This is me, Wesley Cuthand, he thought. I have been on this planet nearly twenty-one years and what the hell do I have to show for it? He pulled the elastic out of his own hair, which immediately flowed around his shoulders. In the old days, he'd once heard, warriors cut off their hair to show they were in mourning. He picked up the purple-handled scissors that were still lying beside the hot-water tap. There was no more mournful time than the present.

11

Lynda stood out on the street with Seth, even though the Sunday morning rain was still coming down hard. She didn't want Del to have to come inside to get them. She didn't want to obligate herself any further than she already had. So she waited in the rain with Seth backed up inside her jacket.

Del appeared not more than three minutes later, just when he'd said he would. All dressed up even though they were only going to the vet's. Before she could reach to open the door of the cab, he was out of the truck and had opened it for her, first lifting Seth inside, then placing his arm under her elbow so that the smell of his aftershave and the sweetness of his gallantry made her go unexpectedly weak at the knees. She made it up into the cab. The door closed. She caught her breath. She couldn't look at him when he arrived back in the driver's seat, but mumbled, "Thanks, Del. This is very nice of you."

At the vet's they were taken back to Tessie's cage. The dog raised her head when she saw them, then laid it heavily back down again. She closed her eyes but her tail thumped a couple of times. They all crouched down so they could be closer to her. Seth spread right out on the floor, stuck his fingers in the cage, and Tessie licked them.

"Hi, girl," he said. "Are you better today?"

The assistant who had taken them to the back wore pale blue, and her long dark hair hung down in a single braid. She said with a sad smile, "You're such a good dog, aren't you, Tess." Then, addressing them all, "Dr. Howard isn't in yet. She called and asked about your dog. I don't think anything's changed much. We'll try to get Tess outside after a while and see if that helps any. You're welcome to stay. It might be several more hours before we can tell you anything though."

"Mom, can't we stay?" Seth asked. "Please?"

"Why don't I take you two out for breakfast?" said Del. "Kill a little time. Then we'll come back."

Again, Lynda was flooded with gratitude. Tessie did not look good at all—listless, woebegone—a dreadful sickly odor rising around her. What if the vet couldn't help her? She'd heard about dogs with perforated bowels. This was serious.

"I don't want to leave her," said Seth, beginning to cry.

"Saw a hockey ball at the hardware store—dollar twenty-nine." Del raised his gaze to Lynda, then back to Seth. "Orange. Might cheer your dog up."

"Yeah?" Seth sniffed and wiped his eyes.

So they went for breakfast, with the promise that they'd stop along the way and buy a get-better-soon present for Tessie. In Del's truck once again, Lynda couldn't help thinking that no matter how things played out, at the end of it all there would be a very expensive vet bill she couldn't possibly deal with. She also thought about how her life, once so full of promise, had descended to this: a pile of bills she couldn't pay, a business she couldn't run, a son who gave her more joy than she was able to give back, and a loneliness so deep that a man fifteen years her senior, with whom she had absolutely nothing in common, could make her feel things she hadn't felt in a very long time.

Noreen awoke to a dull morning. Rain was hitting the roof of Del Armstrong's cottage. Beyond the window, everything dripped. The lake rolled to shore with an insistent breaking thud. In the clammy bedroom she sat in the middle of the bed wrapped in an old quilt and felt her seventeen-year-old spirit being sucked right down to the gloomy bottom of the lake.

She got up and pulled on her socks and remembered that everything she owned, including a fleece pullover that had once been Wesley's, was still at the café. She missed Wesley. Missed him so much she felt a great dividing chasm that could be her heart splitting right down the middle and falling apart. She wondered about this feeling and then realized that, like the sky when it turned pale with stars, as it had last night out on Mary's deck, the Universe was sending her a clear message:

NOREEN STALL
IS DEEPLY, TRULY, AND
TERRIBLY IN LOVE
WITH WESLEY CUTHAND

It was an awful, awful message. It spread across her mind, moved down her body, and came to rest right at the place where that baby, no bigger than her little finger, was curled sleeping, waiting to grow and expand in its own tiny orbit inside her.

She got out of bed and found the bathroom and then walked through to the living room. The bedroom where she had been sleeping, and also the bathroom, felt brand-new—even smelled new. By the gray light of the lake-facing window, however, this section of the cottage looked older. Somebody had tacked up a poster of a guy with long bushy hair playing a guitar—a kind of hippie from the sixties. In fact the whole room was that way, full of old stuff—the big chair by the fireplace completely covered with a ragged Mexican blanket, its long fraying tassels trailing along the blue shag rug; the empty bottle of Suavo tequila, covered with dust, that sat by the hearth; a guitar with only two strings that leaned against one wall.

She sat in the chair, looked down beside it, noticed a cardboard box crammed full of what looked like old photo albums. Reaching inside, she pulled out the one that was the easiest to get at and began to flip through it. Some of the photos were loose, in little piles as if waiting to be pasted in. Also, tucked between the pages, were mementos, such as greeting cards with people's names on them and neatly folded pieces of newspaper that announced things like Mr. and Mrs. So-and-So, along with their daughter, so on and so on.

She flipped quickly through to the back of the album. The colored photos were all faded, people looked washed out. Then, on the last page—as sharp as life—a large black-and-white photo of two young guys waving from a roof. She looked more closely, and felt a shock because she recognized one of them—Del—a really young Del, but you could tell it was him, all right. She leaned over and put the album on the floor, leaving it open at the last photo. Then she sat back and looked at those young faces for a very long time. The other guy must be Del's brother. They sort of looked alike. And he was a lot older—just like Gladys was older than her.

Feeling cold, she thought maybe she would build a fire. She had never made one before, but it couldn't be too hard to do. She got out of the chair, pushed the photo album out of the way with her toe, and lifted off the fire screen. Near the cardboard box, neatly tucked inside a basket, were some rolled-up newspapers and dry sticks. Stacked in an alcove was a load of logs. She scrunched some of the newspaper and shoved it in the fireplace, placed a few sticks on top, added a couple of small logs. That was pretty easy. She found wooden matches on the mantel. After she'd struck five or six and thrown them in, the fire finally took. She stood back to watch it blaze up.

Then something went wrong—the smoke didn't go up the chimney. Instead it began to curl back inside the room. She ran to open a window but couldn't figure out the latch. She tried the next window over. In her panic she couldn't open it either. Smoke had started to fill the place. She desperately tried opening the door leading onto Del's deck. It finally swung wide and the breeze and the rain came sweeping in. Then something crackled behind her. She turned in time to see a line of fire begin to creep along the edge of the Mexican blanket. The cardboard box beside it suddenly ignited. She grabbed the blanket from the chair and began to beat it against the box. Some of the flaming material came away. One piece landed on the rug, another on Del's photo album. She turned wildly around—now the chair was on fire.

Dolores Harper stood by her wood-burning stove—the one Mirella had always insisted she should get rid of, but of course Dolores never ever would. She poked at the dying fire with a long metal prod.

Today marked the anniversary of Mirella's death. She was dreaming a memory of her in the hospital on that final day. In this dream she held thin Mirella, hardly bigger than a sparrow in her bed, and wept and brushed her cheeks in long feathering strokes and said goodbye to her. It was the hardest goodbye she had ever said. Harder than to either of her parents. Harder than to her own sister, so long ago. Even harder than to Raymond, bless him always, Sweet Jesus. Saying goodbye to daughters, she dreamed, must be the hardest and loneliest thing a woman ever has to do.

She dabbed away her tears, replaced the iron plate on the stove top, pulled on her rain jacket, went outside, and stood there sniffing the air. She felt uneasy somehow. A toad clung to the cedar railing on her deck. Blinked at her with murky eyes. Without a moment's further hesitation she left her yard and hurried along, past dripping birches, down the winding deer trails that led to Delbert Armstrong's cottage.

12

Dolores knew something had gone badly wrong. Smoke drifted from the open door. She rushed up the steps and onto the deck. Through the floor-to-ceiling glass she could see Noreen beating back flames. She raced inside, tore off her jacket, and joined in swinging, hitting the fire, smothering it, stamping on it.

"Get water!" she yelled at the terrified girl.

Noreen leaped off to the kitchen, came back with a leaking plastic pail, threw water on everything, and went back for more while Dolores coughed and beat at the fire with her jacket. They at last got most of it under control—the collapsed and smoking cardboard box and its contents, the blackened sections of shag rug, the charred and melted remains of a photo album. But the chair kept flaring up—little licking flames would die off and then suddenly burst anew. The inner coils were probably red-hot.

"We're going to dump this whole thing in the lake," Dolores instructed. "Let's go."

They lifted the smoldering chair, rushed it outside under the dripping sky, heaved it face-first into the rolling waves. Then they stood back to watch as steam drifted up around it.

"What happened?" Dolores managed to ask. "How did all this get started?"

Noreen sank down, legs outstretched like a doll's. "I was cold," she pouted. "I made a fire in the fireplace. The smoke wouldn't go up the chimney."

"Did you open the flue?"

Noreen turned up her frowning face. "What's a flue?"

Dolores rubbed trembling fingers along her forehead and thought that this was a child having a child, who didn't know the first thing about taking care of herself. She thought back to the time when Mirella, also seventeen, had been pregnant. She had had the child, a somber little baby girl with long fingers and toes. She'd given it up, gone on, and grown up. But the thing that had made Mirella glow from the inside out, even through all of her anger and rebellious acts, never did come back. And the boy she had thought she would love forever disappeared into the land of lost loved boys, became a man, and found his own life.

"You could have burned the whole place down," Dolores said. "Fire is a powerful thing. It has to be respected."

"I don't care anymore," Noreen told her angrily. "I just wish I were dead."

"Well, that is some mess you just made," said Dolores, suddenly enraged. "In Delbert's place—that he offered up to you with a good heart! So don't you start telling me about dying! Why can't you think about somebody else for a change? What's wrong with you?" She stopped right then. She was shaking. She'd said enough. This was handling it all wrong.

"I just make trouble," said Noreen. "And I'm going to make trouble for this baby, too." She burst into tears.

Dolores shook her head. It was going to be a long day. In one hour the service over at Pembina Lake United Church would be starting and there was no way on earth she was going to miss it— today of all days she needed to be there. But first she had to get hold of Delbert and tell him he'd better come over and take a look at the damage. She hoped that what had been lost in the fire wasn't too precious to him.

13

Noreen looked down. The fine hairs along her bare arms were singed. The awful smell reminded her that something had just happened that couldn't be fixed. It wasn't so much the destroyed chair or rug—although these were bad enough—it was the burned-up photographs. Especially the one of Del and his brother waving down at some unknown photographer with all of the sky behind them. When she closed her eyes she could still see their uplifted arms and hands, their young man smiles.

Lynda wasn't at home and Del could not be reached. Just now, Dolores had gone back into the kitchen of the Molly Thorvaldson Café to write a note. Apparently after this she and Dolores were going to church.

Noreen sat down to wait on the same stool she'd sat on when she arrived, scared and cold and wet, two nights before. She re-called being out on the highway, windshield wipers clapping back and forth, the terror of being totally lost, the white truck appear-ing in the rain and cutting her off. A sudden wing of blinding water. Losing control. Driving off the road, through a ditch, and miraculously coming up unhurt on the other side. Then finding this town, the café lights beckoning like some weird spacecraft in the darkness.

She buried her face in her hands. She hadn't meant anybody any harm and now look what had happened.

She stood up, went to the window by the door, stared mournfully out at the day. The rain had stopped. The sun had come out, burning heat through the trees, sucking the moisture right back up into the brilliant blue prairie sky. She saw the way this fierce naked light hit the empty street. She saw the sky with its thin line of evaporating clouds and tried to think about herself in the future. But no image would come. There was no image of Noreen Stall, hugely pregnant with Wesley Cuthand's child. Or with a flat stomach, in some other place, with some other guy. Nothing. The emptiness of it all filled her with dread.

Right then and there she wanted to get down on her knees and pray to *something* for help. Except not to a boring old man with a beard, sitting in a chair. But what if God was a woman? What would She look like? Noreen tried to imagine Her. Pictured Her rising up from under the grass, Her head popping out of a hill. Then maybe She would grow tall, Her shoulders rounded with spilling dirt. Her hair would be trees and flowers and long prairie grasses. Her feet would be lakes and rivers and oceans. She would wear a crown of sky, with winds and stars and moon and sun and darkness and planets. She would have a pregnant belly, so big that on stormy days, if you looked up into the sky, you would be inside

Her, inside God, and the lightning flashing across would be Her veins.

She stood there looking out, not seeing the street, but seeing God. There was no one around to share this with. No one to nod and say, "Yes, Noreen. You have seen God. You are having a once-in-a-lifetime vision. If you let it, it could change you forever."

Instead she thought, I don't believe this. This is not happening. Not to me. She lingered by the door, feeling sorry and angry and all kinds of other bad things she couldn't put a name to. Then she stared down at the floor, the dirty wooden planking that had once been part of a living tree, and suddenly thought that the girl inside her, the girl she once had been, was now dead. And she couldn't even begin to think who had taken her place.

part four
STAR

1

A single star, the first to show itself in the northern summer's late evening twilight, shone down on Delbert Armstrong's milk cows and on a cat with five half-grown kittens—none of whom he'd had the heart, this time, to get rid of—who led her little family up through the tall grasses in the roadside ditches toward the barn. This same star also shone brightly down on Wesley Cuthand in Brandon, nursing his fifth beer with his friend Martin, out in Martin's backyard; and upon Del himself, out working late—it was almost eleven o'clock on this warm July night—picking up new-mown bales from the hayfield just east of his barn.

The lumber for the addition to the main deck was still wrapped in plastic in the back of his truck. It had sat there untouched for two days. He had not yet gathered up sufficient heart to go down and take a look at the cottage, but it was time he did. He had to make some kind of decision. He'd called the insurance adjuster, who had called back, and now he was avoiding her. The chair hadn't been anything special. As for the rug, Danny had purchased it for a song—as a second in Brandon—hauling it into the cottage, heaving it onto the floor, rolling it out with a kick and a grin, and then handing Del a cold celebratory beer.

It was the photographs that couldn't be replaced. How do you put a price on a memory that looks back at you—one that is so sharp it stops the world and takes your breath away?

The girl, Noreen, who was back staying at Lynda's, apparently couldn't face him. Wouldn't talk to him. Well, he knew what that kind of shame felt like. He wasn't angry with her. He was just heartsick about losing—what? Images, yes, and of course they didn't bring Danny back. It's just that sometimes, when he'd stared at them hard enough, long enough, things felt normal again.

A south wind stirred the leaves in the cottonwood near where he worked. Then the wind shifted direction, moving in strongly from the east. It carried the thick reedy smell of the lake, and it carried memories. On the morning Danny drowned, when they brought him up from the bottom of the lake, somebody said a small pure white stone had been found in his mouth. Del shivered in spite of the heat, and his loneliness deepened.

2

Tessie now had a bad infection, was on antibiotics, and would have to be closely watched, but she was home. Thank heavens, Dolores thought, she hadn't needed to have surgery. On Sunday morning the bone, by itself, had slipped on through like a charm. Now that that was no longer a problem, everyone else was falling apart. Mary wasn't speaking to her, Del had disappeared and wouldn't answer his calls, and Lynda had pulled even deeper inside her ailing spirit. Noreen—more sullen than ever—was back staying at the café.

Used to be, in the old days, if an old person spoke, everybody would listen—even if that person who was speaking happened to be a fool. Well, she wasn't a fool! Over the past three-quarters of a century she'd picked up a few useful ideas! There had even been a meeting regarding Noreen—and yes, it was Dolores herself who had called everybody together. They didn't have to come but they had, and that just proved how much they all needed to get together on this.

"Let's put it to a vote," she'd said, looking around at them. They were all sitting at the table in the kitchen of the Molly Thorvaldson Café. Noreen was upstairs, hiding in Lynda's office, and couldn't be persuaded to join them.

Mary, of course, couldn't understand why they didn't just boot the girl out of town. Lynda, unblinking, held Seth like a shield on her knee. Del was speechless, and who could blame him. No sooner had he and Lynda come back, surprising them all by bringing Tessie with them, than he was given the news about the fire.

But what they all needed, Dolores felt, was to look at the situation a different way. "Certainly," she had said, "somebody could drive Noreen over to Brandon right now and stick her on a bus.

That would be it. The end of our responsibility. And I'm sure we'd all sleep good just letting her go off like that, feeling like nobody in the world cares enough to make her start taking some responsibility in her own life." She sent this challenge around the room. It glanced off Del and Lynda—who now had her head practically buried in Seth's hair—and Mary. Del was the last to lower his eyes.

"Or," Dolores continued, "we could let her continue on here *at the very least* until the Grey Goose pulls in on Friday. Maybe by then somebody can put some sense into her. Although my vote would be for a longer period." She paused, then added, "She can stay with me."

"Don't be crazy," erupted Mary. "She's a wild girl and a thief! Remember, you're an old woman, for heaven's sake."

"How could I forget with you around to remind me?" Dolores told her sharply.

"That's it. I'm going now." Mary grabbed up her sweater, pushed past them all, and left.

"I'll take Noreen back," Lynda offered wearily. "I was the one who started this in the first place. By taking her in. It's my responsibility to see it through."

Lynda was being ridiculous—she wanted Noreen about as much as she wanted to fly to the moon. Dolores retorted, "Haven't you been listening to me? This doesn't have to fall on your shoulders, Lynda. I'm willing to have a crack at it. In fact I want to. What else do I have to do all day?"

Del leaned forward and stared at his hands. Dolores remembered back to a time when he was not much older than Noreen, about three months after Danny died. She was walking up the road to her place, and there was Del, a skinny lost kid, sitting in the dark on a little knoll just above his brother's cottage. He had a case of beer beside him and was slowly going through it—a quiet drunk—all by himself. She should have gone over right then and put her arms around him and talked to him. She didn't. She kept on walking—like people do when they tell themselves they don't want to interfere but are really too chicken to get in there and help. Fact was, she had failed Del. The whole town had. His mother gone. And now Danny. The father—a good enough person, but taken up by his own grief until he died as well, fifteen years later. And Del finally got sober. He'd managed to get through it all on his own. But now she wasn't going to let them—having taken in Noreen—just throw her away. Human beings were not disposable items. Somebody had to take charge.

Seth struggled away from his mother's grasp, ran over, and sank down beside Tessie, who lay panting on her blanket near the back door.

"I like Noreen," Seth said sadly. "So does Tessie." He looked deeply into the dog's eyes. "Don't you, girl?" He stroked Tessie's head. She slowly thumped her tail.

Lynda looked over at her son. "Would you like Noreen to be with us?"

Seth vigorously nodded his head.

"It's settled then. She can stay here." She looked right at Dolores. "It's only for a few days. It's better this way."

"Well, I'm going now, too," said Dolores, placing her hands on her knees and rising. She picked up her cap and put it backward on her head and told them, "I wanted her to stay with me. Maybe for even longer than a few days. But now, apparently, I am too old to handle renegade girls. And nobody cares to hear that this one is headed for big trouble unless somebody does something real quick."

"Yes, we care," said Lynda. "Don't go—please. It's just that we've got a difficult situation here."

"Please yourselves," said Dolores. "I'm tired. I'm going home."

So here she was now, standing in her own kitchen, sipping her evening tea, looking down at the darkening lake. There were no easy solutions to the Noreen problem. Might as well enjoy the scenery. She loved the way night descended in the summer— so slow it was almost midnight before there was enough darkness for the fireflies to make an impression, their sparks and signals as brief and dazzling as the northern night itself. She took in a long breath, calming herself, reminded as always that God was alive, that miracles could happen, that prayers could be answered.

She picked up her phone and dialed Del's place. She got his answering machine, but spoke into it clearly. "Del," she said, "maybe you are outside. Or maybe you are standing by the phone listening to me. I want to confess to you about a night when you were Noreen's age. Remember after Danny died? Well, I saw you alone. You were drinking. I should have gone over to you. I'm ashamed now that I didn't. And so very very sorry." She paused, collected herself, and continued, "Have you been down to your cottage yet? If you can't face going there by yourself, then I'll go with you. Stop hiding and call me. Please."

3

Noreen walked down the empty street to the lake. She kicked off her shoes and felt the warm water. Looking up at the prairie stars in the vast shimmering sky, she remembered Wesley's words: *As long as you can find the stars, Noreen, or even imagine them, you can convince yourself that you don't feel lonely.*

Earlier in the day when Lynda was taking Seth to this very same beach, Noreen had been invited to tag along. It had been hot and she was bored. She didn't have a swimsuit and wasn't going to ask if she could borrow one. She spread out a shirt that had once belonged to Wesley and sat down on it to watch mother and son bob around in the waves. The dog slowly waded in, stared out into the water, changed its mind about swimming, then listlessly dragged a stick up onto shore, where it lay down again and gnawed away.

Noreen hadn't realized that Del's cottage would be close by—in fact, from where she sat she could practically see through the front windows into the living room. And then there was Del's chair—a little way down the beach and sunk partway into the water—exactly where she and Dolores had heaved it. Reaching into her backpack, she pulled out her sunglasses and put them on and tried to hide inside her own head. The fire was hard to forget. The dog was easier to look at—since yesterday, when they brought it home, it had been steadily improving.

Seth came onto the shore, goose bumps all over his white body, pulled a towel over his head, and sat beside her.

"Don't you like to swim?" he asked.

Noreen ignored this, sat back on her hands.

"My dog is feeling better," he said suddenly, fixing her with an unnerving cold blue gaze.

The kid was becoming a pest. He stretched his feet out in the sand, wiggled his toes, brought his left foot up to examine it. "I had a sliver the other day."

"That's nice," she said.

He lowered his foot slowly and said, "Promise you won't feed her chicken bones again."

"Look," she told him, "I didn't think about how it could make her sick, okay? It wasn't my fault. It was an accident."

"Was the fire an accident?"

"Why don't you go now."

"I want to sit here," said Seth, squinting into the sun.

Under the stars, Noreen pulled her shorts up around her thighs and waded farther in. The water felt good. Del's empty cottage was the only one on the beach. The next nearest, with its warm lights, stood alone in the hills that shouldered the lake. There was nobody around. She returned to shore, peeled down to her bra and underpants, and went right back—diving in, then swimming just beneath the surface. The silky water slipped past her like a dream. Rising again, she took a long slow breath. The nausea that had been coming and going all day gradually eased. The lake cradled her as she bobbed around in the waves. Another deep breath. Curling into the fetal position. Her body sinking, then drifting to the surface in a slow silent arc. Lifting her head into the world above for more air.

After that she swam farther and farther out as she tried to recollect some bond between herself and Amazing. After all, she'd spent nine whole months swimming, more or less, inside her. But this was a disgusting thought. Who would want to spend any more time than they had to with Amazing?

Her arms were growing tired so she turned over and floated on her back under the dazzling night sky. In her mind an image grew—Gladys's face—as clear as seeing her own reflection. Gladys, at fourteen, with her easy smile and good hugs. Gladys, with her arms wrapped protectively around Noreen as they watched TV—and the laughter that came from deep inside her body. Gladys, who had her own life. Gladys, who didn't need to be bothered with a knocked-up stepsister.

Seth came awake from a bad dream—Tessie was lost and couldn't find her way home. Real tears, just like a person's, rolled down her doggy face. He opened his eyes. Shadows flashed on his bedroom wall—Noreen in the hallway, slipping past his open door, slinking quietly downstairs. He listened, then heard her leave the café with the softest shudder of the back door. While his mom slept on in the next room, he pulled on his clothes and his shoes just like a big boy, and after that tiptoed down to the kitchen.

He was so relieved to see Tessie there, snoring by the door—her feet kicking out like she was chasing a dream rabbit—that he knelt down and kissed her. This startled her awake. She got up, shook herself, and stood looking at him sleepily. He was glad she wasn't sick anymore. He opened the door so quietly that it wouldn't even wake up a mouse. Before he thought about it, he was running down the street to the lake, with Tessie trailing along behind him.

When they got to the beach Noreen was nowhere to be seen. A single light on a high pole by the dock shone a little way out into the water. Beyond that he couldn't see anything. Near the dock was a pile of clothing—shorts, a top, a pair of sandals—all of which he recognized as hers.

She'd gone for a swim. She shouldn't do that. You always had to swim with a buddy. He took off his own shoes and stood at the edge of the water, but still he couldn't see anything. Tessie began to bark.

"Stay, girl," he commanded, as the little waves rolled across his feet.

He heard a truck come bouncing down the road, and turned to see it drive onto the beach and beam its lights on him and Tessie. He fell down, struggled to get to his feet again—his jeans soaked through—and suddenly Del was there, lifting him up, yelling at him. He was so startled he began to cry.

"What are you doing here?" Del shouted into his face. "Where is your mother?"

"Noreen!" Seth cried all the harder and pointed into the dark water.

"Noreen? Out there—in the lake?"

Seth began to sob. "I followed her . . . that's all . . . Del."

Del held him close and began to call, shouting her name. Soon Seth began shouting for her, too, high in the big man's arms.

"I can't swim," Del said at last.

Seth rubbed his eyes. "I can't either."

Looking out into the dark lake, Seth had the scariest feeling of all—that you could get lost and be lost forever, and nobody would know where to come and find you.

"Oh my God, there she is!" Del cried suddenly.

Finally Seth saw her, too, moving like a ghost, walking slowly under the night sky with no moon. Only stars to light her way.

4

Noreen trailed after them to shore, where she snatched up her clothes. Seth watched while she got dressed. Del lowered his head and walked away. By the time she sat down on the beach shivering, Del was back with a jacket for Seth and an old blanket for her that he'd retrieved from the back of his truck—heavy and scratchy when he placed it around her shoulders, and smelling strongly of fuel oil.

"You could have compromised the boy's safety," Del said angrily. "Didn't you know he'd followed you?"

Noreen looked at them both in shock. "I had no idea he was here. I'm sorry." She didn't know. And she was sorry. How could he think that?

"You're sure about that?"

"Yes! Cripesake—I'm not a monster. Even though everybody in this jerk-ass town seems to think I am."

"Watch your language there," said Del, but he relaxed slightly. He came and sat close to her, with Seth wedged protectively between them. The dog came along, too, crowding in, sitting on her feet, not budging even when Noreen tried to push it away.

"I swam out too far," she explained, because that seemed to be what they were waiting to hear.

"Why did you do that, Noreen?" asked Seth.

She didn't answer. She could feel every shiver of his skinny little body. The dog got up and moved a few feet away, finally settling down on the sand.

Del looked out at the water, fingered a cigarette from his shirt pocket, and struck a wooden match with the edge of his thumbnail. He lit the cigarette, inhaling hard, and said, "Lost a brother. About a half mile out into the lake. Right off this beach."

Seth twisted around and looked up at him. "You should never smoke, Del."

Noreen lifted her head from her knees. "You lost a brother?"

She wondered—had that been the guy in the photograph? The one on the roof with Del?

Del inhaled again, flicked an ash onto his soggy shoe, smoothed it over with a thumb. "Drowned."

"Your brother drowned?" said Seth. "Is he dead?"

"Of course he's dead," snapped Noreen.

"Oh. Are you sad, Del?"

Del said nothing and stared out into the water. After a while, he spoke. "Later his fiancée, Vera, and I . . . we stood here. And right out there . . . see?" He pointed off to some invisible place. "That's where they'd dropped anchor. Danny and her. Swimming off Vera's dad's boat. Thirty-five years ago next week." He nodded his head. Went silent.

The heavy blanket made Noreen want to throw up; she hated the smell. But she didn't move. She waited for Del to continue. In a weird, awful way, this waiting was the same as what had always happened whenever Wesley had recounted the story of their love—slowly, so that not just his words were important, but also the long spaces between them—as if he was trying to understand something and he wanted her to understand it, too.

Del crushed the cigarette carefully on his shoe. He tucked the butt in his shirt pocket and turned to her. "Vera told me he dove into the water and never came up again. His last words to her were, 'Tell that SOB brother of mine I hate his guts.' Excuse my language, Seth."

Seth leaned against Noreen. She wrapped up more tightly inside the blanket. Lowering her face, she wiped at the water that still dripped from her hair, and, shocked, looked Del's way. "Your brother actually said that?"

"Guess he'd found out something he shouldn't." He stared straight ahead again, his profile strangely lit by the single light overhead in the beach's only lamppost. White moths and fish flies batted against its bulb, flew off, vanished. "I'd been secretly holding hands, you see," he continued softly, "with his Vera."

"Holding hands?" Noreen absorbed this—his delicate choice of words with their feel of betrayal. "Oh," she said. Then, "Oh," again.

Del let out a strangulated sound. Was it a sob? She looked quickly away. The wind picked up a swirl of sand. She heard it sifting through the night air just before it blew across her face, stinging her eyes, filling her mouth. She spat away grit, threw off the suffocating blanket. It was a terrible story. Even more terrible was the fact that he had shared it with her. She didn't know what to do with it.

"I'm sorry about your cottage," she blurted at last. "But it wasn't my fault. I didn't mean for all your pictures to get burned up. It just happened. I mean, I lit that fire in the fireplace and everything just went wrong all of a sudden." She paused, wiping her eyes, and continued in a trembling voice, "It's the story of my goddamn life, Del. I can never do anything right."

"Crazy dream—for a farm boy—a summer cottage by the lake," Del said, as if he hadn't heard, or didn't care. "But it was Danny's dream. Not mine. Even though I never seem to be finished with it . . ." He stopped there, voice trailing away.

Noreen dug her toes into the clammy sand. No adult in her life had ever spoken to her this way, so broken and full of guilt.

"I'm cold," said Seth. "Can I go home?"

"Of course you can." Del was now blowing his nose. "We'll take you there straight away."

But he remained sitting, as if he couldn't move just yet, and Noreen didn't move either. The unease of what she had done to Del—of what that lost picture of his brother and him in happier times must have meant—was settling in again, and it wouldn't go away.

"Are we leaving now?" said Seth.

"Yup," Del told him, still not moving.

Noreen waited, too—for something.

Del drew in an audible breath and let out a ragged, "So. What *were* you doing—way out there in the lake?"

"Thinking."

"Thinking?"

Testing stupid fate. Just wanting—something. "Nobody gives a damn," she said miserably.

"I see." Del looked down at his feet. Squinted out at the water. "That rug of mine will very likely need replacing. And the chair."

"I've got some money," she said quickly. "You can have it. All of it."

"I won't accept your money." Slowly nodding his head, he added, "However . . . there *is* something you can do. For Lynda." He picked up the cast-off blanket and rose to his feet. Seth and Tessie immediately started for the truck. Noreen stayed in the sand, still waiting.

Del stood over her. "I've got a proverb for you. It's from the Spanish. Goes something like this: *Take what you want. And pay for it.*" Cold tears glittered in his eyes. "Isn't that a humdinger?"

5

Del still hadn't gone into the cottage. He had meant to. But then the thing with Noreen and Seth. He'd gotten them both back safely to the café and then had a talk with Noreen. A couple or so weeks of pitching in at the café, he figured, was not a lot to ask. As long as she kept quiet about where the help was coming from, and kept a record of her hours, he didn't care how she handled the rest of it with Lynda. That was up to her to figure out.

After leaving Lynda's café, he drove over to Tiger Lily hill and sat in the silent night, all the windows rolled down—even the frogs and the crickets had gone to sleep—with only the wind for company. It was lonely, this life he was living. Had been for quite some time now. The fire only proved that. What did he really have to show for all these years he'd been trying to find his way back to being a good person?

He remembered Vera—the smell of her. And her laughter. The distinct thrill of knowing how wrong it was, what they were doing. And then the shock of watching his big brother sitting out by the barn, when he found out about them. Sunk down, the sweat still clinging to his strong arms, looking up from his hands at Del—the chill of not knowing what he would do next.

Danny disappeared that day. Went to find Vera. To confront her. But when he took her out on the lake, she didn't know a thing was wrong until he turned in a rage and gave her that message just before he dove off the boat.

Del drove slowly back to the farm. He got out of his truck and went inside and snapped on all the lights. It was three in the morning. What he really wanted was a drink. Instead he sat heavily by the phone and listened to his messages—two. First the insurance adjuster. She was nothing, if not persistent. Then Dolores—her voice as soft as a mother's lullaby, telling him how sorry she was for coming upon him when he was seventeen, just after Danny's death, drinking alone by the lake—and not doing anything about it. He couldn't even remember that night. There had been so many of them. He erased the first message. He played Dolores's message again. Five times. Each time he pulled in a little more strength. And then a little more. It didn't really solve anything, but it did take the edge off wanting that drink.

6

Tuesday morning Noreen got up, dressed, ate a piece of dry toast, drank some orange juice, struggled with rising nausea, and lost the battle. After that she washed her face in the cramped bathroom with the ugly waddling-duck wallpaper and came back out into the kitchen. She wanted to go upstairs and sink back down on the cot and forget the whole thing. Last night outside the café in

Del's truck, she'd given her word, with Seth, half asleep, as their only witness. Maybe she didn't really have to do this.

Lynda had been sleeping soundly when they got back, dead to the world, her snores coming out in short little rasps. She could now be seen in the café, pouring coffee for some saggy-assed man.

At the table Seth played tiredly with bits of cereal that bobbed around on a sea of milk in a pink plastic bowl. Noreen felt a twinge of sympathy. This was short-lived. As soon as he noticed she was back from throwing up, he started in, his annoying little voice heavy with meaning. "You *said* you were going to talk to my mom."

"Lay off, okay? I just tossed my breakfast."

"When will you talk to her?"

"Whenever."

"I don't believe you." He lifted his spoon, let the milk slowly splash back into the bowl.

Noreen folded her arms tightly across her chest and said, "And I don't care. I really don't. I don't give a rat's ass about anything."

Seth slowly got down from his chair. He dragged his feet to the main entrance of the café and stood there, head hung low. "I'll tell her myself," he said, not turning around.

"Oh, for Pete's sake! Go back and finish your cereal."

She went to find Lynda. Something had spilled, then been allowed to dry on the café floor. Her sandals gripped the sticky spot. She stood, feeling trapped, wondering how she was going to do this, all the while watching Lynda make another pot of coffee. Finally she just muttered, "I want to work for you."

"What?" Lynda's wiry curls, wet with perspiration or maybe still damp from her shower, stuck to the sides of her face.

Noreen repeated it loudly and slowly: "I said, I want to work for you."

"Good luck," muttered Lynda.

She followed Lynda back into the kitchen, embarrassed that she was doing this. This begging crap. "Yeah?" she managed. "Well, I'm serious."

"So am I." Lynda shoved a mop into a pail of soapy water, leaned on the handle, and looked straight into Noreen's eyes with her own red ones. "Nobody makes a living in this town. It's full of old people who've got no money. The few young ones who do have some spend their working days and their paychecks up at Willow Point. I can hardly afford to pay myself, Noreen. What makes you think I could hire you?"

"You don't have to pay me." Even as she said it she wanted to fly off somewhere. Run outside, flag down a passing car.

"What brought this on?" said Lynda in disbelief. "You and I both know I can't have you working for nothing."

"Okay—so I don't need money for a while," Noreen continued, her voice wavering. "Wesley handed me some back before he left. It's mine to do what I want with. He told me to keep it."

"Really." Lynda puffed out her cheeks. "How admirable. And what's that got to do with anything?"

"What's wrong with you, anyway?" said Noreen, anger flaring again. "I need a cheap place to sack out for a while. And you need a waitress. Do we have a deal, or what?"

Last night Del had said, "Keep track of your time. Whatever it comes to—at six dollars an hour—goes indirectly to paying me back. Understand?" He must have the hots for Lynda or something. That was the only thing she could think of that would make him ask her to do something as strange as this.

Lynda sighed and said, "Look, I *am* sorry for you. I mean that, Noreen. When I was a teacher there wasn't a single day went by that I didn't look up from my desk and see, well, that my students needed a lot more from me than I had to give . . ." Her voice trailed away.

"A teacher? You were a teacher?" Lynda sure didn't look like one. "What happened to you?"

Lynda blushed—except not the kind of blush you have when you're a little bit embarrassed. This was the kind that comes from the heat of shame and fear inside your life. For the second time that morning, Noreen felt a rise of sympathy.

Finally Lynda met her eyes again, and said evenly, "I could use the help. I have to start doing things differently around here."

Noreen felt ill once more, and not just from morning sickness. Her life—a nothing—and this baby she and Wesley had made without knowing or caring that they were making it—it was a nothing, too. And even if she turned her back on this whole mess—even if, right this minute, she bolted out the door—truth was she had nowhere to go.

Lynda began to say something, stopped, shook her head, carried on some kind of inner argument. Then, "Okay, here's the thing. I don't know how long you're planning on staying. A couple of days is one thing, but . . ." She looked at Seth, who was now standing beside them, unblinking. "You want to go outside, honey?"

"No," said Seth.

"Well, do it anyway. We're having a grownup conversation here. And take Tessie with you. She needs you to help her get stronger, all right?"

Seth gave his mother a sunny smile and ran to get Tessie.

After he left, Lynda said in a half whisper, "I'm having a hard time making a go of things. Sometimes even just buying food for the café is difficult. Do you get that?"

Noreen looked at the floor. Nodded.

"So it won't come as a surprise that I'd have to ask you for some kind of money for expenses—not a lot—but how about eighty bucks? That would cover your food here for . . . let's say . . . the month. Maybe by then you'll have a better idea of what you want to do with your life. Honestly, Noreen, I can't swing it any other way. Now I've got a huge vet bill to pay off and I was already up to my eyes in debt. It just never ends."

Noreen went straight upstairs, hauled her backpack out from under the bed, plunged her hand inside, found a pen and a Mickey Mouse watch and her tattered notebook from high school that had never been written in. She opened to the first page. Checked the time. Quickly wrote: *DEBT TO DELBERT. Day One. I just spent a half hour trying to convince Lynda to let me work for her FOR NOTHING!!! and now she wants money for food and stuff and says I owe her <u>EIGHTY DOLLARS!!</u>*

She closed the book. Replaced it in her backpack. Counted out almost half of Wesley's money, now hers, soon to be Lynda's. She was so upset she couldn't think straight. It was going to be one horrible day.

7

First the café floor needed scrubbing. Not much later Lynda placed four frozen berry pies in the oven. One of them exploded. Syrupy blackened goop splashed everywhere, causing tiny fires, and the whole oven had to be cleaned. After that the dishwasher broke down—and every single dish, piece of cutlery, and pot had to be washed by hand in stinging water with soap and bleach. Then there was a crisis with Seth, who went out on the street and got into a fight with two older boys.

"They took my Blue Bombers cap," Seth sobbed. "The one that Auntie Dolores gave me."

Noreen didn't wait for Lynda to react. She marched outside and told them to give it back. The taller one, who looked around eleven, said, "You're a cow."

"Right," she replied. "And I'm going to kick your ass."

"Oh yeah—well, you're so tough I'm really scared." He said this while looking at her breasts.

Noreen rolled her eyes. She calmly took his arm and twisted it, hard, behind his back, until he released the cap. After that she told them both to piss off.

As they came back inside, Seth clutched his cap and said, "You're strong."

"Stay away from asshole losers," warned Noreen.

"Don't swear," Seth told her with a frown.

She placed her hand on the back of his head. His hair was unexpectedly soft. She felt a lump rise in her throat. He turned his head up—his eyes were so clear. Did every little kid have clear eyes? When did they start to get muddied up?

"I'm really really bored, Noreen," he whispered tragically.

In about thirty seconds he'd be crying again. "Okay, okay, okay," she said. "See all that cutlery there by the sink? Go and dry it and take a long time doing it and stay out of trouble."

Seth beamed, ran over, and grabbed up a towel. "Then can I put them away?"

"*Yes—gawd!*"

A few minutes later, when she walked from the kitchen into the café, the same boys who had picked on Seth were ordering hamburgers from Lynda.

"I'll make the burgers," she said, taking Lynda aside. "I used to work at a burger place."

"Okay," said Lynda uncertainly. But it was lunchtime and she was busy making sandwiches for a group of ladies who wanted takeout so they could go and watch the pelicans on the lake.

When Lynda wasn't looking, Noreen scooped up the crisply fried burgers, spat with slow accuracy on each one, patted them into buns, and brought them to the boys, who smiled foolishly at her. "Have a really nice day," she said, smiling back.

By evening Noreen felt more tired than she could ever remember. She couldn't believe how many customers she had served or how little money was in the till. Thing was, nobody bought much of anything. No wonder Lynda was broke. And as for tips, forget it—a grand total of four dollars and seventy-one cents. Old people with shaky hands would get up from having pie and coffee, leaving a dime or a couple of nickels and a few pennies beside their gucky plates.

Just before closing time Del came into the café, took off his hat, and ordered a cup of coffee. She slid the cup across the counter. He picked it up and sipped it, scalding hot, set it down carefully, and asked for a burger. She wanted to be mad at him for making her be there, but all she could see was his drowned brother, wet and silent, weighing him down.

She went straight to the kitchen and cooked up his burger with care, putting extra dill pickles on it, some thinly sliced onions, a bit of horseradish, some mustard and ketchup and mayo, a piece of smoky cheddar, and a big slice of tomato. She stuck a toothpick in it to keep the top half from sliding off. She brought it to him, then watched as he took a bite. His eyes lit up.

That was it. Nothing else. Not a thank-you. After he'd paid and left, she looked under his plate. Nothing there, either.

Deflated, she went back into the kitchen. Lynda looked at her for a moment, stiff-mouthed, then said, "Hungry?" For the first time in days, Noreen replied that she was.

Lynda held out an apple in her white freckled fingers. "This is mostly what I ate for the first three months I was pregnant with Seth."

Noreen took the apple, ripped off the little label that said New Zealand, Royal Gala, bit into it. She sacked out on a chair and said, "Were you married to Seth's dad?"

Lynda looked away. "His father is no longer in the picture. And bringing up a child on your own is harder than you can imagine."

"What happened? Did he beat the crap out of you?" Noreen bit off another chunk of apple, slowly chewed, waited.

Lynda came over, leaned against the table, and said bitterly, "What else do you want to eat?"

"Wow—*sor*-ry. He must have been a real prince."

"My ex-husband is not up for discussion."

"Right." Noreen rolled the apple around on the table. Lynda was still glaring at her. "Don't look at me like I just killed your kid. I'm just trying to figure out what your problem is."

Lynda nodded. "So," she said. Then, "So," again, and nodded her head several more times—like she was dumbfounded. She switched on the stove, angrily banged around, getting out a pot, filling it with water. She dumped in a box of macaroni and slammed down the lid. "I hope you like macaroni and cheese," she mumbled.

"Love it," said Noreen.

Lynda turned to her again. "So." It seemed to be her favorite word. "Are you planning on keeping that baby you're carrying?"

Prickles of humiliation settled right down at the exact place where the baby floated. "I have no idea. I'm waiting to see what happens."

"The baby won't wait," said Lynda.

"Well, that's *my* problem, isn't it!" Noreen got up and swiftly left the table.

Del.

10:00 o'clock <u>in the morning</u> until 9:45 AT NIGHT. (She would have stopped there but she needed to rant. Her pen whipped along the page.) *Do I count in the time I spend NOT telling my so-called boss to take a fricking leap? I'll NEVER be like her. And by the way thanks for the generous tip. That really topped off my super day. Signing off, Noreen.*

8

Dolores got out of bed at five o'clock on Wednesday morning. The birds had barely shaken themselves from sleep. She walked down to the lake to gather some wild mint—before the sun rose and burned off the dew. She liked to think in the early morning. It seemed at this time of day, the ancestors were so close you could speak to them. Strange that her own daughter was one of them now. Well, here came the sun—peeking up over the hills at the other side of the lake—fiery peach swathed in lavender clouds. What a glorious sight! She spied some Saskatoon berries on her way down to the lake. They were plumping up real good. Soon she'd be making pies again. She chuckled to herself. She had made so many Saskatoon pies in her lifetime that if you laid them all out they'd stretch from here to Brandon.

Del attended to his morning chores. After that he got into the truck and drove down to the cottage. He was feeling strong enough to do this today. He appreciated how kind Dolores had been—her offer, left on his answering machine, to come with him. But this was a private duty.

First of all, when he walked inside, he could smell it—that there had been a fire—and then the living room, of course, didn't look the same. The chair was gone. Black patches burned into the rug. Soggy bits of scorched photographs and paper everywhere. The albums, most of them, burned beyond recognition. He rifled through the pages of the only one that had somehow survived. There were the early pictures of the family—very early, he was a baby. Danny's birth certificate: Daniel Carruthers Armstrong. Their parents' wedding photo. Nothing much left. He was surprised at how little remained.

Near the fireplace he discovered another album—hard to tell which one it was—so badly burned the only thing remaining was the plastic covering, shriveled by the heat and melted into the carpet. He felt an urgent need to leave, to be anywhere but here.

He walked out onto the deck, then down to the lake. Danny's old chair—reeds caught in the scorched fabric, their tendrils floating out into the water—looked like a washed-up creature. Pulling off boots and socks, rolling up his cuffs, he waded in and dragged it back up onto the beach. He sat down beside it, looked out into the water. Trailed his hand along the sand. His fingers came across a cold stone. He picked it up, stared at it. It was as white as a lily. Pure as death. He put it in his mouth, felt it on his tongue, spat it out, and wept.

9

Noreen woke up that morning with a pain deep inside her which came and went. In the bathroom she discovered spotting on her underpants. It scared her so much that she called Lynda.

"Where is the pain?" Lynda's face crinkled in a kind of dry alarm, right along her brows.

"It's on my left—lower side." She couldn't stop shaking.

Half an hour later, after Dolores had been called to come in and take care of Seth and the café, she and Lynda were in the car on their way to Willow Point, where Lynda had managed to get an emergency appointment with her own doctor.

"I didn't think about anything going wrong," said Noreen. And then she fell silent.

"Bound to be a few twinges you aren't used to." Lynda reached over and lightly touched her hand. Noreen felt the shock of skin on skin.

"Look," Lynda continued, "forget what I said yesterday. I was in a foul mood. It's not your fault that my life is falling apart."

"I've had lots of boyfriends. But I have never been pregnant. *Never.*" She yanked down her sleeves and hid her hands inside them. "My stepsister, Gladys, took care of me and then I took care of myself. I'm not stupid. I'm not some pathetic loser you have to feel sorry for. So why don't *you* forget it."

Lynda frowned. "Where was your mother?"

"Drunk, or working," said Noreen. She could see this remark registered with Lynda, that she got it—that somebody got something, finally.

They pulled into Willow Point. With renewed panic she asked, "Will you go with me into the doctor's office?"

"You mean when she examines you?"

"Yeah."

"Never had an internal before?"

She wondered if it would hurt, but she couldn't bring herself to ask. "No. I haven't."

They walked into the clinic together. She was given forms to fill out that asked embarrassing questions. The internal was mortifying and it stung. But afterward the doctor told her she was about seven weeks along, and probably things were okay with the fetus—it might just be her ovary causing the pain—and that she would need an ultrasound, on an urgent basis, right across the street at the hospital.

It was the ultrasound that was the most amazing thing. Not only was everything going to be okay, but there was a tiny white blip that kept flashing on the screen. It came from the fetus, curled up snug as a little peanut inside her.

"That's the heartbeat? Oh, my God." She looked up at the technician, who was smiling, and at Lynda, whose eyes had misted over.

"It's good and strong," she was told. "Your pregnancy looks fine."

Some cramping was considered normal, and the odd bit of spotting, too, as long as it didn't increase. She should see the doctor in another month. That was it. And her Manitoba Medical covered everything. In the meantime, she was underweight and anemic and needed to start eating properly and take iron pills. They stopped at the local pharmacy and after that they headed back for Pembina Lake.

All the way, Noreen held her stomach. She was stunned. The baby was real—not that she hadn't thought it was real. It's just that now she'd seen it. And most incredible of all was its heartbeat—flashing like a little star in the universe of her tummy. She felt unexpectedly proud. And scared. She started to wonder if maybe she should call Wesley. It was confirmed. No way it could be anybody's baby but his. He should know about this. And Gladys—maybe she should call her, too.

In the end she didn't call anybody. What would she say after she told them?

Dolores stayed on at the café into the evening. Before leaving, putting on her cap, folding her battered black purse tightly under one arm, she said, "Noreen, you take it easy now. Go to bed soon. And here—" She pulled the lid from a little plastic tub and held it out. "Take a good whiff."

The strong smell of mint rose from a damp bouquet of bright green leaves nestled against paper towels.

"Medicine. I just gathered it this morning," she explained. "It's mint. Grows wild by the lake. Make it into a tea and drink it—slowly. It's good for all kinds of women's things. And"—she paused, shifted her weight—"don't just toss the leaves into the garbage after you are through with them. Bury them by a tree. Let the earth take them back." Smiling, she patted Noreen's astonished face and then left by the back door, whistling a tuneless song.

Noreen drew the wild herbs up to her nose. They smelled like regular mint—except stronger and somehow sharper. The smell alone made her feel calm. She said to Lynda, "I guess if it's for women it can't hurt."

Lynda folded her arms and smiled down at her feet. "She likes to help out. It cheers her up. I'm glad. She's been good to me. And she's had a hard time."

"What kind of hard time?"

"Lost her daughter. Cancer. Last summer. So—will we make you some tea?"

Back in her room later, with the window open wide and the breeze blowing in that smelled of the lake, Noreen began to write up her report, but soon put down her pen. So many things had happened that day.

At the end of it all, right after fishing the soggy mint leaves from her teacup, she'd taken them outside to bury them, just like Dolores said, in Lynda's yard behind the café. When she was sitting on the ground digging up a little patch with a spoon beneath the biggest tree—a broad willow—the upturned earth smelled like spring and mud pies. She wondered if the baby inside her was a girl.

She picked up her pen and tried again: *Del. I guess you know that Dolores had a daughter who died of cancer last summer? If cancer were a person I'd kick it right up the goddamn ass. Signing off, Noreen. P.S.—I worked from around noon until closing.*

10

On Friday, Noreen served two people who straggled in for coffee and pie at around three o'clock. After that there was nothing. For the past two days there had been a pretty good breakfast crowd, but by lunchtime there would be only a few customers and the afternoons and evenings were totally dead. Three flies buzzed annoyingly around on the countertop. Seth had been banished to the backyard, where he played camping with Tessie—a game that involved bedsheets for a tent, dried macaroni, and some pots of cold water.

"Ever think about taking down the wallpaper?" Noreen asked, half asleep, chin in her hands.

Lynda lifted her head from the day-old city newspaper she'd bought across the street at Shore's Groceries, looked over at the peeling wallpaper in the corner above the back booth, and returned to doing the crosswords. "Thought about it," she said into the newspaper, and penciled COMPASS into 19 across. "I have thought about a lot of things over the past three and a half years."

"I'd do it for you. Then paint your walls."

Lynda picked up her coffee, slurped it, made a face as if it was bitter—it probably was—and put down her mug. "Would take a lot of paint."

"Paint can't cost that much. Come on, live a little." Noreen gave her a nudge.

Lynda grunted as if something was giving her indigestion and sank back from the paper. She slowly rolled her head one way, then the other, wincing as if in pain. "I'm not exactly sure what's under that wallpaper. I'm afraid to look."

"I'm not." Noreen got off the stool, which wobbled and squeaked behind her. She walked briskly over to the back booth, stood on the seat, reached up and grabbed the peeling wallpaper, yanked hard once, then again.

A huge piece, heavy with old plaster, suddenly gave way, exploding in a spray of powdery chunks, knocking her to the floor.

She sat there, aghast, as the dust rose in a white cloud, then fell. A gaping hole over the booth revealed electrical wires hanging between old boards. She staggered up and spun around to face a horrified Lynda.

11

Del sat down to a meal of wieners and warmed-up canned beans. He looked around his cramped farm kitchen, noticing it for the first time in years. He suddenly realized that he hated it. In fact he hated this entire house—his old family home—and always had. It was plain ugly.

He tried to think back to a time in his life when he'd been happy. Really, nothing had made him happier and prouder than the work he and Danny had done on the cottage, building it from scratch. As they'd worked, Danny talked about leaving the farm, becoming a carpenter, and wanting him to finish up his last year of high school so that they could start something together—a little construction business maybe. Instead life changed. Nothing got started. It all, now, seemed like so much driftwood.

Still, he felt better today than he had on Wednesday evening, just before Dolores suddenly appeared down at the cottage. He'd gone away for a while, then come back and was standing in the living room, wondering if he was a fool for keeping the place. Why not pack it all in? Forget the insurance adjuster, throw down a new rug, call a real estate agent, and sell the place. Get rid of it once and for all.

And then there was Dolores—peering in at him, tapping at the glass on the deck door—when he really hadn't wanted to see anybody. She'd caught him. He had no choice but to go and let her in.

"Well, Delbert," she said, pushing past him, "I promised myself I'd come by to help you clean things up—and I see I'm not too late. Let's have coffee and then we'll get started."

A few minutes later, sitting across from him at the kitchen table, she looked up at the pale green walls and said, "You did some beautiful work in here. I like the cupboards. This kitchen looks brand-new."

Nodding, he allowed that it was.

"So you should do the same with Danny's living room," she continued, looking into her cup, swirling the liquid around. "Too many memories anyway."

Dolores, he was learning, had a way of making you think, of uncovering ideas that were already in your head—ideas that you hadn't yet dared to acknowledge.

12

Silence filled the café. Lynda disappeared in her car, taking Seth and Tessie with her—leaving no instructions, saying nothing about the huge piece of plaster that had fallen away from the back wall. She just got up, her face suddenly colorless, and left without a word.

Noreen stood looking at the rubble. How was she to know this would happen? The wall was obviously rotten or something. Well, she'd clean up. She could at least do that. She went into the kitchen, found a trash bag, came back, and started to fill it up. When she lifted it, however, the contents were so heavy that everything broke right through the plastic and hit the floor. Ghostly dust rose again, got into her lungs, made her cough. Her teeth were gritty and her eyes itched. Outside, behind the café, she found an empty container, brought it in, started over.

No doubt about it—the hole over the booth spelled trouble. It yawned accusingly and she felt that accusation the whole time as she swept up the final bits of debris, filled a pail with hot sudsy water, brought it back, and started to scrub everything down. She was in the middle of scrubbing when the Grey Goose bus pulled up and braked to a stop, the motor still running. The blistering smell of diesel fumes followed the bus driver, a young guy, as he strode into the café. She could see a few passengers staring past streaky windows, anxious to go again, waiting for him to get back.

"Pack of smokes." He pointed to the kind he wanted, then turned and did a double take as he noticed the wall. "What happened there?"

"We had an accident," Noreen told him, and went to get his cigarettes.

He gave a low whistle. He smelled strongly of cologne and there was a tiny but brilliant diamond in his ear. "Cool," he drawled. "Must have been fun to watch."

"Very funny," she said.

"Nobody taking a trip today?" He handed her a twenty.

She made change. Dropped it into the heat of his smooth hand. Looked over his shoulder at what was left of the wall. She thought about how she would be blamed for this new disaster. There was no way around it. Lynda had watched the whole thing happen.

She took a deep breath. "How much," she asked, "is a one-way ticket to . . . wherever you're going?"

13

Lynda left Seth and Tessie in the car, walked up to the back door of Del's farmhouse, and knocked so hard the wood rattled. He appeared seconds later, smoothing down his hair when he saw her, ushering her into his kitchen, smiling, offering her coffee, a chair, was she hungry? He looked past his window to her car. Why didn't she let Tessie out and bring Seth in?

She stood in the middle of his quiet kitchen—the summer wind blowing around them through the open door and around the house—and heard the bellowing of one of his cows off in a field somewhere. She could feel Del's eyes on her, and his kindness. She went silent for a long time while he waited, not moving, not rushing her to speak. At last she said, "Something happened at the café. I guess it's making me want to give up. But I thought, first—before I decide to do that—maybe I'd come here. And see you. To . . . ask for your help."

14

Noreen climbed on board the bus. It hadn't taken more than five minutes to shove all her things into her backpack and the plastic bag she had arrived with. She swung down the aisle and into an empty seat as the bus pulled out of town.

"Next stop, Willow Point," the driver called, his deep sleepy voice reaching all the way to the back.

Noreen sank low, put her feet up on the seat in front of her, and watched the town of Pembina Lake slip away. She had a few twenties left of Wesley's money and a bit of spare change, and no idea what she would do next. High up over the road, the rolling wheels of the bus beneath her, all she wanted was just this moment—no thought, no plan.

She pulled a multigrain bar out of her pack—one of the purchases she'd made when she and Lynda had stopped in at the pharmacy after her visit to the doctor—and peeled back the wrapper, bit off a chunk, chewed, swallowed. After a couple of bites, however, the swaying of the bus made her sick. She stuffed the bar back into her pack. A baby over in the opposite seat began to wail. She watched as the mother lifted her shirt. The kid latched onto her breast and started to nurse.

This whole baby thing was so unnerving. She looked away and thought about Wesley. She'd probably never see him again. She had been so bad to him.

She stared out the window. The scenery was now whizzing by—all full of the greens of summer—the farmers' fields, the grassy ponds, the valley hills they had just begun to climb. Then quite suddenly she spied two vehicles as they pulled up on a side road and stopped at the junction of the highway. She recognized both—Lynda's red hatchback and Del's green truck. The bus slid past them and she stretched her neck, watching until they were no longer visible. The driver opened a window and stuck out his elbow. The baby, groggy in his mother's arms, finished nursing.

An overwhelming urge to just get off the goddamn bus overtook Noreen. Grabbing up her things, she jumped out of her seat and careened past startled passengers until she reached the front.

"Let me off," she said to the driver.

"Here?" he said to the road. "This isn't a designated stop."

"I don't care." She threw him a poisonous look. "Frickin' stop this bus right now and let me off."

His eyes traveled quickly to her, then back to the road. "I'm not giving you back your money. You bought the ticket. Understand?"

"I don't give a shit. Do *you* understand?"

He shrugged, slowed, braked to a halt, and let her off.

Feet on the road, she slung her pack low on her spine, and the bag containing the rest of her belongings over her shoulder. The air smelled perfumey with plants. Of course it was a dumb idea—going back to finish out her time as Lynda's lackey. And they'd all hate her now. But to hell with everybody. She was going to do it anyway. The low sun shone in her eyes. It was going to be a long hot walk.

15

"Water damage," said Del. "See?" He pointed up at the hole. "Take a look at that lathe. Even from here you can tell those boards are rotten, nails are all rusty. Maybe this old building's shifted, too. But . . ."

Lynda folded her arms across her chest, couldn't believe what she was hearing, wondered how much this was all going to cost. Damn that kid anyway—and where was she? The café door had been left wide open and not a trace of her.

"Seth," she said, "will you go upstairs, please, and tell Noreen to get down here right now?"

Seth, hauling Tessie by the collar, went to find Noreen.

"Don't be too hard on the girl," Del continued. "Sooner or later this would have happened, anyway. Just poor timing is all." He wiped his hand across his lower chin. "I'll probably have to check the roof. The problem may have started there." He looked solemn, like a doctor who was preparing to give some very bad news.

"I'm sunk in the water here, aren't I," she said heavily. "So tell me, please, and let's get it over with."

"Thing is," he ventured delicately, "I've got all kinds of building supplies, Lynda. Just kicking around." He paused, folded his own arms, looked at her, looked away again. "I could . . . help. Just like you asked."

Seth came back then, and she distractedly laid her palm on his thin little shoulders.

"Mom," said Seth, breaking into her thoughts. "Noreen's gone."

"What do you mean—gone?" She looked down into his innocent eyes and thought that maybe he hadn't checked properly. Then she remembered, through everything that had happened, that it was Friday—that the bus pulled into town every Friday and in ten minutes was gone again, like a dream you thought you'd had and were still trying to remember. Well, yes, Noreen just might be on that bus right now, rolling through the hills on her way to God-knows-where.

She felt relieved, then angry. And then—this was the surprising thing—disappointed.

16

The first thing Noreen saw when she got back to town was Del standing up on Lynda's roof. She dropped her belongings at the side of the café. She was sticky and hot and wanted a goddamn shower right now. But there was Del, looking down at her. Well, shit, she thought, and raised her arm in a halfhearted wave. He didn't wave back. Stood instead, hands on hips, the early evening July sun still hanging with dog-day heat and determination behind him.

"Thought you took off on us," he said.

"Yeah, I'll bet." She was back now, and if they didn't like it, screw them. She'd keep right on doing what she'd stuck around to do here in the first place.

Del said nothing, hunkered down on the roof, and peeled back a piece of shingling. It came away in his hand. He tossed it over the edge. It sailed quickly to the ground.

"Look," said Noreen, hating his silent treatment, "I'm back, aren't I? And it took me two fricking hours! I walked the whole goddamn way!"

"Well, good for you," said Del at last. "Go on in and talk to Lynda."

The booths had been pulled away from the wall. The hole was larger than when she had left because somebody had gone in there and knocked away a whole bunch more plaster. Lynda stood in the middle of the café, a broom in one hand, a bucket in the other. Dolores—sitting at the table nearest the kitchen—held Seth on her knee. She pursed her lips in a disapproving way when she saw Noreen come through the door and looked over at Lynda.

"Where have you been?" Lynda demanded—like it was any of her business.

"Out," Noreen replied.

"*Out?* Have you any idea what you started here? Have you any idea what a . . . a screwup you are?"

Noreen slumped down in the empty chair near Dolores and waited it out while Lynda railed at her—yelling about walls being knocked down and drywall that had to be put up and painting that would have to be done and a section of roof that would need to be torn up and then replaced and how none of it would be done by tomorrow and Saturday was her only good day of the week and she might as well throw in the towel right now, and what did Noreen intend to do about it?

"Why do you have to close tomorrow?" said Noreen. "People will come in anyway and we'll sell them pancakes and it'll give them something to talk about."

Dolores nodded, silent but more or less agreeing, and patted Seth's bare knees.

"Take a look around you!" shouted Lynda. "Can't you even for a minute stop and consider the repercussions of this mess you've gotten me into?"

She was obviously too upset, too crazy with anger, to even be spoken to. So Noreen didn't bother. She went behind the counter, poured herself a glass of water, knocked it back, wiped her mouth with her gritty hand.

"If you'll excuse me," she said coldly, "I'm going outside to help Del."

The screen door slammed behind her. She walked out and looked up, but couldn't see him on the roof. She went into the side yard. Del had just started to climb down an extension ladder that rested against the building.

"A quarter of this roof needs reshingling," he said, feet scraping and rattling hollowly on the metal rungs. "Take about a day to do."

"Well, I'm going to help you," Noreen said emphatically.

He reached the bottom, turned, threw his hat down by the side of the building, wiped the sweat from his forehead. "Only if you agree to listen to me. You can't just go waltzing around a potentially dangerous place. Some of that wood has rotted right through."

"How hard can it be to fix a roof?" She wanted to climb up and stand on top—to be there right now with the sky at her back—to get started using hammer and nails. It would feel so free. Like you were a bird.

Del shot her a hard look. "You damn well better not go up

there," he said slowly, "unless you're *with* somebody. It's time you stopped acting like an impulsive little kid. Even Seth has more common sense than you do."

Deflated, she watched as he carefully released the sections of ladder, picked it up, placed it on its side against the café, then walked through the uncut grass and dandelions to his truck. Over his shoulder, he offered, "I've got quite a few things to round up at the cottage. I'll have to load it all so that I can start here first thing in the morning. You'd be welcome to tag along. I'd be glad for the company."

She didn't want to go to his cottage, didn't want to go back to the scene of her last screwup. But at this moment, even though she could still feel the sting of his words, she wanted to be with him—so what else could she do?

17

Noreen rolled over in bed—the morning light stabbed her eyes—and reached into her bag, pulling out the multigrain bar she had started to eat on the bus. It was important to have better nutrition, the doctor had said. Until she made some kind of decision she could at least try to do that. She pulled back the wrapper, took a bite. Chewed. Swallowed. Gladys always used to say things looked better in the morning. Most of the time Noreen felt her stepsister was dead wrong about that.

She shifted around, pulling herself up so her head rested

against the wall behind her pillow. A bottle of orange juice sat on the floor beside her cot. Where had that come from? She picked it up, twisted off the top, took a long cool pull. She noticed that she didn't feel nauseated for the first time in a long while. Even her breasts, which had been so tender just a couple of days ago, felt fine. She wondered if this was normal—if certain pregnancy symptoms just went away after a while. Well, it was probably the minty medicine Dolores had given her. Maybe she should ask her for some more. She finished the bar, drew her legs up, froglike, beneath the blankets, and enjoyed this new feeling of ease. The pale blue top she'd slept in sloped like a piece of sky over her body. She stroked her abdomen, right about where the baby would be, and breathed slowly in, then out.

The door to Lynda's office creaked open slightly. In the space she could see small eyes beading at her.

"Stop spying on me."

Giggles from outside the door.

"Okay, come in if you want to."

Seth, wearing Del's cowboy hat, came bounding into the room with Tessie close behind.

"Where did that dog come from!" she yelled. "Get her out of here!"

Tessie wasn't listening. She clambered up onto the bed. Seth, too, knocking Del's hat onto the floor. The dog lowered her muzzle onto her paws and wagged her tail. Seth shoved himself down under the covers, looked intently up at her, and said, "I'm glad you came back, Noreen."

His wholehearted manner shamed her. After all, here he was—just a kid—a little person who was in the world and wanting somebody's attention just like anyone else. She'd spent most of her time until now trying to ignore him.

Lifting her arm, she drew him close. His hair smelled of shampoo. He snuggled happily against her and said, patting her stomach, "Auntie Dolores says you're going to have a baby. Are you?"

"Yes."

His small hand rested on her stomach. "Is it a girl baby—or a boy baby?"

"I don't know. I think maybe it's a girl." Noreen leaned her head heavily against the wall behind her and felt like weeping. Maybe it was her hormones. She took a deep breath and said distractedly, "Where is your mother?"

"Downstairs. And I'm bored, bored, bored." Seth gave a little shuddering sigh.

Noreen's head snapped forward. "Is the café open? Is she opening it today?"

"Yes, and she won't let me help."

"Don't lean against me now." She pulled herself up straighter. "Is Del here yet? Bugger off, okay? I have to get dressed."

"I don't want to bugger off. I want to stay here with you." He slid down until the quilt fell over his face.

Noreen pulled back the covers. "Go."

Seth reluctantly slid away, bare feet hitting the floor. He picked up Del's hat, put it on his head, went over, and pulled at Tessie.

The dog grunted, then galumphed off the bed, too, and disappeared out into the hallway. But Seth, still by the door, not leaving, nervously twisted and untwisted his fingers. Suddenly, he put his hand to his grinning mouth, blew her a wet kiss, and dashed out of the room.

She rolled over and dug her watch out of her backpack—it was ten minutes to seven. Del would be here soon. She smelled coffee brewing, heard the whine of the side door opening and then Dolores's voice below, talking to Lynda. She pulled on pants and a shirt and sneakers and hurried downstairs to face the day.

Shreds of ancient wallpaper and chipped plaster and bare inner wall showed behind the booths, which had been temporarily pushed back into place. Seth was leaping and running through the middle of the room, darting around the tables already set for breakfast.

"Outside! Right now!" Lynda ordered.

Seth came to a dead stop, looked over at Noreen, and started up again.

"I'm open for business," Lynda told Noreen, with an accusing look at the open wall—not noticing her son's small act of defiance.

"Bugger. Bugger. Bugger. Bugger," chanted Seth as he picked up speed.

Lynda stood, hands on her hips, glaring at Noreen. "And thanks for your charming influence on my son's social graces."

Del clattered through the door just then, three paint pails dangling from each hand. Seth pushed past him, Tessie in tow.

"I found your hat, Del!" Seth pronounced as he disappeared into the summer day.

"And how are you two ladies this morning?" Del asked carefully, nodding first to Noreen—who rolled her eyes—then to Lynda.

Lynda responded by lifting her arms and furiously pulling the elastic out of her hair, shaking it, shoving it back into an oddly beautiful clump, and winding the elastic around it again. "Do you want some coffee?"

"Guess so."

For just a split second he seemed to wonder if he should leave. But instead he put down the pails and stood firm—as if nothing on earth was more important than this moment.

And then, in a single star-bright flash, Noreen realized three things. First, that as small and depressing as this town was, people stuck around and cared for each other. Second, that Del, no kidding, was pretty much gone on Lynda. Stranger still—and body language does not lie—there was something powerful going on within Lynda too. Third thing was that, without some major help, these two people would never make it into the sack.

"But don't bother making any," said Del, like a dumbfounded, thunderstruck man. "Coffee. If it isn't made."

Lynda quickly flushed and lowered her eyes. "Of course it's made. This is a café. Coffee is always made."

A steady stream of customers came and went beneath them all morning as Noreen and Del, on the roof, ripped away a section of old shingles and sawed through rotten wood, tossing everything over the edge of the café into the side yard. You could see the whole valley from Lynda's rooftop—the lake that glistened and rolled away to the south and the treetops buffeted by the damp breeze that rippled up through town.

They worked steadily—Del was worried about rain. This all had to be done by nighttime. She did everything he told her to do in exactly the way he told her to do it, and they didn't talk much, they just worked. By noon they were down to exposed rafters. They stopped to have lunch out on the front steps. After that, Del cut some sheets of plywood to fit and they took it up top. He gave her a hammer and showed her how to line everything up and drive in the nails. Next came the sheets of tar paper, cut to measure, overlapped, stapled into place. By early evening when they came down to grab a hamburger, they were ready to put in the metal flashing and then lay down the shingles.

At ten o'clock that night Noreen followed Del out to his truck and poked her head in the passenger's side window. "I've been writing those reports," she told him, "just like you asked."

"That's good." He gave her a curt nod. "Keep writing them." His hand was on the key.

"And I'm paying her for food and stuff." She opened the door quickly, got inside the cab, and slammed the door shut. He looked at her in alarm.

"I'm a total screwup. So shoot me." She played with a piece of torn plastic that frilled up around the door lock. Then she flopped her head back on the seat. "Look—I didn't mean her any harm. Can I tell you something else?"

"What is that?" His whole attention was on her now—something of a smile starting to grow on his face.

"If I tell you this—one messed-up person to another—promise you won't get mad and hate me."

"I'll try," he said, with what sounded like a small chuckle.

"It was me who almost killed her stupid dog."

There, that did it. Smile gone. Like the moon behind a cloud.

"Tessie? You mean Tessie?"

"Yeah, Tessie. I didn't do it on purpose. I just gave her that chicken bone because she was being annoying. Begging. It was late. I'd just gotten here—first night. So I'm in a strange place and I've just taken my boyfriend's truck and his money and on top of that I'm pretty sure I'm knocked up. Which, of course, I now know I am. I wasn't exactly thinking about how I could almost explode some dog's guts."

"Noreen, girl," he managed finally. "You are a funny kid. Have you always been this way? Walking from one disaster to another?"

"It's not funny," she said miserably.

"I'm not laughing." He reached over and gently patted her shoulder. "Go inside now. We've got another busy day coming up. And it appears you are sleeping for two."

She got out and watched him back up onto the street. He waved to her—held his hand high—as he drove away.

Del.

When my mother, Amazing (don't ask—I've mostly always called her that, and believe me she's hardly Amazing) finally found somebody who would marry her, she promised me, Honey, things are going to go good for us now. Stupidhead, her soon-to-be husband, would take us out for dinners all the time and his twelve-year-old daughter Gladys would look across the table at him like she couldn't believe what she was seeing. I remember that look on her face. And don't tell me I was too young to have that kind of memory. Some memories are as sharp as knives, as you and I both know.

So I want to know, how can I bring a baby into this crummy world? Signing off, Noreen.

18

At a construction site just south of Brandon, Wesley took off his hard hat, wiped the sweat from his forehead, and walked toward his truck. His best friend, Martin LaTourelle, tall, skinny, with the face of an innocent child and a mind as restless as a Saskatchewan thunderstorm, sauntered along behind him, taking one last drag on his cigarette. No smoking inside Wesley's truck—the little tag hanging from his rearview mirror said so. Everybody joked about it, since everybody but Wesley smoked, but they all honored his wishes. They might all have tried—and succeeded at one time or another—to screw his old girlfriend, Chantelle, but the no-smoking thing was firm.

Nobody at his construction company, for obvious reasons, had ever been introduced to Noreen. But they all knew she was the reason he had cut off his hair. So they offered him beer. They told him jokes. They kept him up until three in the morning when they had to be at work early the next day. All to distract him. But nothing was working.

Martin swung his grasshopper legs up beside Wesley in the cab of his truck and they headed back to Brandon.

"Well, bud," said Martin. "You want to hang at my house for a while?"

"Naw, think I'll try and get some sleep."

"How about Sunday? Spend the day together. What do you say? Drive up to Clear Lake. Go for a swim—catch a few rays. C'mon, it'll be great."

"I'll think about it."

"You really should call her, you know. Maybe she's still at that place. Pregnant and all with your kid. What happens if she decides to have it? Then your baby will be growing up with some family you don't even know."

"She already told me," said Wesley. "She's having an abortion."

"Really. That's what they all say. Some do. Some don't. Ones that don't are the ones that are hung up on you. That's been my experience."

Wesley snorted and looked dejectedly out on the prairies. Fiery red and purple light descending. He rolled down his window to sniff at the night air. Sweet, like clover. He sighed. Why couldn't women be sweet like that?

19

Dolores Harper couldn't sleep. Delbert over at Lynda's café until all hours fixing up another calamity that Noreen had set off. Lynda herself so angry with the girl that she had lost perspective. They'd had, when all was said and done, a very good Saturday. Noreen had been right—that punched-away wall certainly gave people something to talk about. And joke about. There'd been more customers than the three previous Saturdays put together— not only for breakfast, but also in considerable numbers for the full-course noonday meal. And it went on like that right through a hungry supper crowd. People loved trouble—loved it, of course, when it was somebody else's. But when Lynda tallied up all her overflowing cash at the end of the day, she still had a real sour face, and that was a puzzling thing.

Then there was Mary, who had never even shown up, as was her custom on Saturday afternoons. When Dolores had called her up to find out if she was all right, she'd gotten the phone slammed down in her ear. In all their long years of friendship Mary had never done anything like that. So final. So unkind.

She reached over and snapped on the light, swung stiff legs out of bed, shoved sockless feet into a pair of slippers. Didn't bother taking off her pajamas—just pulled a sweater and a pair of fleece pants over them. She paused by the mirror to pat down her hair. Who was that person in there? Wrinkled skin that used to be velvety. Sunken eyes. Oh well, Dolores, you just got old. You had your time to be young.

At the back door she lifted her jacket from its hook and left the house. The air smelled good and she breathed it in deeply. The Creator, after all, gave us the magic of crickets singing in the darkness, soft nights and sighing trees, universal skies with their message of stars.

Mary's porch light beamed brightly, so maybe she was still awake. They'd both always been night owls. Dolores walked past Mary's fifteen-year-old car—curled-up oak leaves from last fall still clinging to the windshield wipers. That's how long it was since they'd been out driving together. Since Mary had been behind the wheel of her car. Well, it was time to have a little conversation about that, too. Time to get things out in the open.

Dolores knocked on the door and, as there was no answer, stepped inside. The house smelled as if the garbage hadn't been removed for several days. When she walked into the living room, she found Mary asleep in front of the TV. Oprah was talking to Dr. Phil McGraw and their guests about the children of bad relationships. It must be a tape—Oprah would be in bed by now. She picked up Mary's remote and pressed the reverse button. Dr. Phil and Oprah slid back in time to the beginning of their conversation. But Mary, slack-mouthed beside her, a gravy-stained white sweater buttoned up wrong, a paper towel hanging like a flag from one buttonhole, was snoring loud enough so it was hard to hear unless she turned up the sound.

So she sat and watched the silent images roll by. Dr. Phil leaning forward, fingers pressed prayerfully together. Coming to his point, whatever it was. Oprah attentive in her deep-hearted way. It was good when people talked the truth and showed that they cared about each other. She wished that people really behaved that way. Nobody, it seemed these days, was interested in having truthful conversations. Unless, of course, you faced them up to the unpleasant facts. Which was a lot of work. And made your heart tired.

She reached over and poked Mary awake. She had been drooling in her sleep. Dolores pulled the paper towel from her sweater and dabbed at Mary's chin, because that's what good friends did for each other. Then, thrusting the towel back into Mary's open hand, she spoke solemnly into her fully awake and startled face. "We need to talk. Maybe there is something you need to tell me about. Maybe, until now, I didn't want to hear it. Maybe, for quite some time now, since Mirella died, my own heart has been dead to you."

Mary sat up straight in her chair, fumbled with the buttons on her sweater, undid them all slowly. Did them up again properly. She scratched at the gravy stain. She folded her hands, rubbed the thumb of her left along the knuckles of her right.

At last she said, "I had a stroke last fall. Small one, the doctor said. It happened while I was out driving—you weren't with me that day. It was only a couple of months after you had lost Mirella and what with everything that was going on it just didn't seem right to say anything and I didn't want to worry you."

"Oh," whispered Dolores. "Oh, dear."

"And that's all I'm going to say, Dolly. Let's not make a fuss about this." Mary released her grip on her own two hands, then began to run them rhythmically along the arms of her chair.

Oprah and Dr. Phil had finished their conversation. The credits were rolling. Dolores settled back in her chair to sit with her friend. Later she'd get up and wash Mary's dishes and take out her garbage and make them some tea. Then they'd sit some more—maybe even until night tilted into morning. Just like the old days. A couple of sister stones, watching the warm July sun rise up.

20

Noreen broke off working with Del to go outside and yell at Seth, who had been on the other side of the door with a plastic swatter, bashing flies so hard against the screen that one whole corner had come jaggedly loose—black mesh fluttering in the morning air—and now they would have to fix that, too.

Seth disappeared around the other side of the building, playing games by hiding on her. She gave up and came back inside. Just as she was sweeping more plaster off the floor, Dolores and Mary walked into the café. The wind skittered in after them, followed by Seth. Dropping the swatter, he threw his arms around Dolores's skirted leg and her hand came down to cup his cheek.

Without turning around, Del said, "Morning, Dolores. Mary. Maybe you ladies could attend to our boy. He's been a little jumpy this morning. Noreen and I are just getting ready to put up the drywall."

Since eight o'clock that morning, when Del had arrived and pulled the booths away from the wall, they had been in behind there with saws and hammers opening things up—floor to ceiling—gradually moving down the wall until he found the beam he was looking for.

"We can't stay," said Mary, a red plastic purse clutched by her side. "But we'll take Seth with us to church."

"We can be here for a while. We've got time," said Dolores, looking over at their work. With a little smile, she turned to Noreen. "I've been meaning to ask you about your condition, Pumpkin—since you saw the doctor. Any more symptoms?"

Mary, who stood by looking Noreen up and down, then turned to Seth. "Are you ready for church? Where's your mother?"

"My mom is very very tired. She went back to bed."

Bang, he ran outside again—then slap slap slap at the flies.

"Coffee's hot, if you want some," Del said. "It's free today."

Mary clasped her hands together, set her shoulders, nodded a couple of times like she was deciding something. "Right then," she said. "Excuse me—I'm going to check on Lynda." She disappeared through the kitchen door.

Noreen grabbed Dolores's arm, felt her soft old crinkly skin, pulled her aside, looked her straight in the eyes. "I don't even have morning sickness anymore. And I wanted to ask you," lowering her voice so Del wouldn't hear, "you know, even my breasts don't hurt like they did and is that okay? Did that medicine you gave me work? Is that what happened? I just want to know. Like, if I'm okay and everything."

Dolores stood back, frowning. "Wasn't the medicine that did all that. You need to slow down some, Pumpkin."

"Really?" Unwelcome tears welled up in her eyes. "Lynda hates me. And this wasn't my fault. Not really. It just happened. All I did was pull some paper off the wall."

"She told me you're working for her now," said Dolores. "Pretty soon she won't need an old waitress like me. She's got a young one to do everything."

"Oh, she's not paying me," Noreen blurted.

Dolores twisted her head, surprised. "Not paying you? She never said anything about that."

"Look," said Noreen, anger rising. "Don't worry. I don't want your stupid job. I never intended on staying." She threw a look at Del, at the back of his head.

"Done here, pretty much," he said, turning around. "Now we can put up that drywall."

Dolores shook her finger at them both—gnarly, Noreen noticed, like an old stick. "What's up with you two? You look like a couple of crows sitting on a wire. Same message."

Del wiped his hands on his jeans and seemed about to say something.

"Nothing's up," Noreen said quickly. It was nobody's business but hers and Del's. "We have to fix the wall. And then we have to plaster it. And then we have to sand it. And then we're going to paint this whole damn room. That's what's up."

"That all sounds pretty good to me," said Dolores. "So why's Lynda still so upset?"

"Beats me."

"She's tired," Del told them. "She'll come around."

Later, outside, as they took a break, Del squinted thoughtfully into the top branches of the big willow across the street at Shore's Groceries. He set his drink down on the cement step between his feet and suddenly said, "Your debt to me is paid in full. You can stick around if you want to. But that's up to you."

Noreen watched a yellow truck. It came from the direction of the lake. From far away it had looked brand shiny new. Now, as it drove slowly past, the farmer lifting his hand in a kind of wave, Del lifting his own in response, she noticed that the fender had rust spots. All in all it looked pretty banged up. From the back of the truck a large dog with matted fur barked at them. Then the truck rumbled across the railway tracks and disappeared like a mirage down the highway.

She twisted the lid of her drink half a turn, looked at Del. "You don't want me around?"

He returned her look. "I didn't say that. And you know it. Don't pick a fight where none is intended. All I'm saying is I don't think I was doing you any favors by keeping you here. I see that now. I was just trying to do the right thing by you. By . . . Lynda." He said the name caressingly, like it was a beautiful word. Yes, he had a bad case of her, all right.

"You're not keeping me here," she said at last, folding her

hands between her knees, watching a bug climb up through a crack in the sidewalk. "I came back. Remember?"

Del left early—the drywall fitted and hammered into place, the plastering done—saying he'd be back first thing tomorrow to sand, and then they could get down to painting the room. Seth was apparently staying the rest of the day and the night at Dolores's—Lynda had left a note propped against the saltshaker on the kitchen table.

Noreen went upstairs. The bedroom door was ajar—as if Lynda wasn't sure whether or not she wanted company. Noreen didn't care what she wanted. She swung the door wide and entered without knocking. Lynda was sitting up reading. She still hadn't changed out of her dressing gown.

"I don't care what you think of me," Noreen started in, "and you can think whatever the hell you want. But Del is crazy about you. And he's crazy about Seth. If you give him half a chance you won't be sorry. But if you don't, well then, you *deserve* to be lonely and old. And be without a man who could love you. And *be without sex for the rest of your life!*"

She left Lynda still staring into her book, speechless, probably pissed off. Who knew? She slammed the bedroom door so hard the wall shuddered. After that she went outside and crossed the street to the pay phone at Shore's Groceries.

21

Wesley got home from spending the day at Clear Lake with Martin. He checked his messages. There were three—more than usual. The first was from his sister Cindy, who lived in Edmonton. She was calling to check that he was okay, as she sometimes did on Sundays, sounding cheerful, the way sisters do when they don't know what's going on with you, but whatever it is they suspect the worst. Then there was a message from his landlord, reminding him that his rent was a week overdue. The last message, however, made him lose all feeling in his legs. He half sat, half fell onto the sofa. Noreen's voice—clear as if she were standing right in the room, searing him with the heartbreaking delicacy of her breath—floated out from the speaker.

"Wesley," she said, "it's me, Noreen. I'm still here at Pembina Lake. If you are the man I think you are, you will understand that I had to get to this point . . . where I am sincerely sorry for all the crap that has happened between us . . . that I personally caused . . . and that I now realize how much . . . how much I *need* to apologize to you. In person would be nice . . ."

She actually sounded kind of grownup. And she wanted to see him—wanted to apologize. She had seen a star on a screen that was a heartbeat. She had seen an image of their baby.

He got into his truck and made the trip over to Pembina Lake in forty-five minutes when it should have taken him closer to an hour. He bumped over the railway tracks that crossed the highway just before town and looked down the street that was pretty much devoid of cars except for two parked in front of the grocery store. He looked over at the café and everything there seemed to be shut down. Even the blinds were closed. He pulled in and parked.

He had to admit that he still felt angry and aggrieved. He was ready to turn around and leave if she didn't have something pretty convincing to say. He'd had enough of this heartbreak shit and who the hell needed that? But as he sat there quietly, wondering what to do next, he also realized that his hope was huge—as if he had reached the sun-dappled shores of a good dream and was resting there, dazzled.

22

Noreen had gone back to her room after leaving that message for Wesley and closed her eyes and pictured the apartment in Brandon. Maybe he'd get home and stand by the answering machine and hear her message and want to come to see her. But then, sitting on the saggy cot—with Lynda down the hall still wrapped in her own loneliness—she had started to worry. Maybe he didn't care. At any rate, it had been impossible to just sit there and wait for whatever was going to happen. So she'd left the café and walked out into the sun and gone down to the beach.

Once there, her feelings had started to ease. Del's cottage

looked almost peaceful in the afternoon light. Someone had lifted his burned chair and set it upright on shore facing out toward the water. Waves broke nearby, washing up shale and debris and threads of water weeds mixed with foam. Gulls flew freely overhead. A dog barked somewhere. She began to concentrate on the sun and haze, the thud of green-and-gold water, the hillsides rolling down into the basin of the valley. Time passing—the afternoon drifting away. Life and time and the afternoon. And her heart beating. And that other little heart beating away inside her.

She had been dozing and she didn't know for how long. All she knew was the lowering sun still clung to the day and she felt hungry. So she got up slowly and started walking back to Lynda's. As she walked along she talked to the baby, who, she had decided, should at least be given a temporary name.

"Your father doesn't give a damn about you, Star," she complained out loud, loving the sound of the name as it floated on the air. "He is a selfish bastard."

Then she thought about Wesley's sweet-smelling hair. His nimble fingers. The way his bare back had always looked irresistible in the morning sunlight. The way, before, his patience with her, his taking care of her, had often made her feel sad and irritated and even sometimes happy, all at the same time.

As she turned onto the main street—the sound of the lake a whisper behind her, the leaves of the tall trees now talking overhead—she saw his truck parked in front of the café and Wesley sitting inside it. She almost didn't recognize him. He had cut his long hair—it was even shorter than hers!

He didn't seem to notice as she got closer, his eyes closed—as if he was concentrating on something. With her hand on her stomach, she steadied herself. The window on the passenger's side was open and she could see the distinct curve of his dark lashes as they rested against his cheek.

"Wesley," she said quietly.

Coming to with a start, he looked right at her. Well, he's angry, for sure, she thought. But at least he's here. At least he came all this way to see me, and that's something. Maybe he doesn't hate me. Maybe there is a chance I'll think of the right words to say to him.

He quickly opened the door, got out of the truck, and stood, hands in his pockets, looking over her shoulder toward the lake. She moved slightly away, leaning back against the cab door. Confusion and sweetness and a heavy ache moved slowly up her body.

When she thought she could no longer stand it, he finally asked, "So have you been out walking?"

"I came from down by the lake and I'm working at Lynda's now and I'm not sure what I'll do after that," she told him all in a rush.

He watched her steadily. She felt a hot sting of shame. She wanted to hide. But in Pembina Lake, beside a truck, in front of a café, wheat fields and sky flaming pink and orange and gold all around, there was absolutely nowhere to go.

"I'm sorry," she said at last, with great dignity. "Sorry for what I did to you."

"Well, that's why I came all this way, I guess . . . to hear that," said Wesley. Then, kicking at the ground, "So you're okay?"

"I've been better. But I'm all right, I guess. Thanks for asking."

Still staring at the ground, "And the . . . baby's okay?"

"Star is fine, too," she said.

Lifting his eyes, "You've named it Star?"

Not it, *her*, she wanted to say. But she had no proof. Just a feeling. "It's just a temporary name. I'm seven weeks along—seven weeks," she repeated meaningfully.

"Lucky number seven. Well, that's . . ."

He looked away, seemingly unable to go on. After a long while he returned her gaze, his eyes filled with naked misery and longing and regret. Looking just the way she felt.

"Can I hold you, Noreen?" he asked. "Would that be okay?"

23

Wesley woke up at six o'clock the following morning. He pushed back the pink quilt from the cramped little cot where they'd been curled up sleeping. They'd sneaked up the stairs together last night. He had to be at his job site on the other side of Brandon by seven. He lifted Noreen's arm—which had been flung in sleep across his chest—and sat up. She murmured and turned over. He would have let her sleep on, but what with everything that had happened since his arrival, he wanted to look into her eyes one more time before he left, just to make sure that he and she were really tight again. So he gently stroked her hair, what was left of it, brushing the raggedy wisps away from her forehead. Pretty soon she opened her eyes, startled.

"It's me," he said with a chuckle.

"Oh," she said, sitting up. "You're still here."

"I've missed you," he said. "You always were the prettiest sight first thing in the morning."

She leaned in and kissed him, then sat back looking pale and serious, with two little frown lines between her eyebrows. This was the face of a different Noreen. Something about her new look made him feel uneasy and insecure. His heart slowly began to sink. It was the look women get sometimes, when they've had enough of you and are preparing to tell you to shove off.

24

Noreen stood beside Wesley's truck. She let him hold her hand, which he didn't seem to want to release, as if somehow she might fly away.

"Do you love me?" he asked. "I have to know. What was that all about last night, if you don't? What was the damn point?"

Here it was again, that old shameful feeling of wanting to run. She had to stop doing this, had to find a way of keeping solid and rooted to the earth. She took in a lungful of damp morning air, letting it out again slowly.

Wesley whispered, "If you don't love me, then I'll leave you alone, I promise. I'm a man of my word. And I won't come back. I'm sick of this old runaround, Noreen, and I'm not going to put up with it. So tell me right now."

Her chest hurt. Last night, after they made love and it had felt so good, she lay there until she heard his even breathing, which meant he was asleep. She had put her hands on her stomach and tried to imagine how it would feel when his baby started to move inside her. But she couldn't. And now she couldn't, either, tell him what he needed to hear.

In front of Lynda's café, Wesley finally let her go. "You have my phone number," he said formally. "So you call me if you ever need anything. I think that's best. How am I doing so far? Tell me, please, because I'm dying here."

She leaned inside the window and kissed him on the lips one last time, long and deep and bittersweet, then drew back. "I guess I can't love anybody, Wesley."

He looked at her with big wide eyes as the sun lifted, gleaming, from behind a mountain of clouds. "That's bullshit, and you know it," he said. "I look at that pretty starry sky you made just for me. I stare up at it every single night before I try to get to sleep. But you break people's hearts, Noreen, you really do, and I wonder if that's ever going to change." Then he backed up and drove the hell out of town.

All the windows in the café were open when she got back inside, and she soon noticed Lynda, still tousled from sleep but dressed—a long thin sweater pulled over a pair of jeans, a dish of vanilla ice cream in her hand.

"I woke up early," Lynda said sheepishly, resting her spoon at the edge of the dish.

"I got up early, too," Noreen said, wondering what Lynda had seen or heard.

"It's okay. I know who was here. I've been awake since four and I saw his truck parked out on the street. That's not what kept me awake. I've just been thinking, is all. Do you want some coffee or something? It'll warm us both up. I just made a pot." She set her ice cream down and went behind the counter.

Noreen pulled her hands up inside the sleeves of Wesley's old blue fleece, sat, and watched as Lynda took her time pouring out the coffee.

"White death," Lynda said with a tiny smile, setting the mug in front of her, pushing the sugar forward. "Remember? That's one of the first things you said to me. That night," she continued, falsely cheerful, as if this were a really great memory, "the night you came here. How long ago? Twelve, thirteen days?"

"More like ten." Noreen poured sugar onto her spoon.

"Time, huh? It tricks you. Doesn't really seem so long ago that I was the same age as you. But it was twenty years ago. Mom brought me up by herself. Do you know she dressed like a . . . I don't know, like some kind of genuine free spirit, anyway. She taught in the high school up at Willow Point. She and the former owner of this place had this strange on-and-off-again romance. He was so much older, but he outlived her. Can you imagine?"

Lynda stopped, then continued with a bright smile. "There's some things you wouldn't ever think about happening. And then they do. Do you know he left me this place in his will?"

Noreen kept loading on the sugar—stopped pouring at spoonful number seven. And then the truth slowly dropped into her head—about what it was that Lynda actually meant by all this soggy revisiting of the past. "I get it," she said out loud. "You're leaving, right?"

Lynda's eyes registered a kind of stunned surprise. "I'm thinking about it." Looking away. "How did you know?"

"Lucky guess."

Lynda met her eyes once again. "I can't do this anymore. I simply can't. Maybe I should go back and teach and have a decent life."

"What a total crock," Noreen said into Lynda's startled face. "I meant every single word I said last night. You want to run away and be a teacher? Well, that's just plain dumb. Where will it get you? Del's crazy about you—in case you weren't listening the first time. He's seen you at your worst and yet he still comes around." She watched Lynda's face slowly color up—burn in little mottles right up her neck behind all those freckles. "And what about Seth? Del's almost like his dad or something. And Dolores and Mary—they're like his grannies."

"I don't know . . . I guess . . ." Lynda seemed completely flustered now, didn't know what to do with her hands. Didn't know where to look. Her eyes puddled up with tears. She said brokenly, "It's my birthday today."

"So—we'll celebrate."

"And I'm a ripe old thirty-seven."

"That's pretty old, but nothing to be ashamed of."

"And I'm so damn depressed and lonely."

Noreen reached to pull a paper napkin out of the dispenser. It fluttered like a bird in her hand. "Don't do this, Lynda," she told her. "Don't run off. I can tell you from personal experience that if you do, you'll be really sorry."

25

Tessie walked slowly in front of Seth and Mary and Dolores, her tail wagging, tongue hanging out of her mouth. Noreen watched the little procession come up the street and thought life was so strange you couldn't bet on anything. Who knew she'd be standing here on a broken-down sidewalk beside a seriously depressed ex-high-school teacher in a crappy little town, watching a badly dressed farmer unload something from the back of his truck—all the while hoping, whatever it was, this surprise of his would help turn things around for everybody before it was too late.

Seth ran excitedly ahead. "What have you got? What have you got! Show me, too!"

"Stand back now, Seth," said Del. "I have something here for your mother."

Dolores and Mary and Tessie caught up just as Del eased a long thin cardboard box down from his truck. He lifted it upright and set it onto the sidewalk and said, "Okay now, Seth, help me open this up. We'll have ourselves a regular unveiling."

Once out of the box, with the paper ripped away, the contents were revealed as a sign. Hand-painted in dark blue on a white background, it said: LYNDA'S—THE PLACE TO EAT.

"Hope you don't mind the name change," said Del. "All due respect to your ancestor Molly Thorvaldson—she's in the past. You're the future."

Noreen, standing beside Lynda, blinked at Del. His smile seemed happy enough, but his eyes were uncertain.

"That's just great, Del. It's beautiful," Noreen declared passionately, because nobody had said anything. Not even Dolores, who just stood there, waiting, it seemed, for something to happen.

Del had stopped looking at everybody. "Joe Vandenberghe's handiwork. Told him it was a rush job. Paint's barely dry." He brushed the sign with his fingers.

"Mom," Seth pleaded, "will you please tell him you like it?"

Lynda managed, "Thank you." But then she reached out and brushed it, too—slowly, with her freckled fingers.

Del looked over at Noreen, then back at Lynda. He took off his hat and slapped it against his pant leg, and smiled. "Any rate—Happy Birthday, Lynda."

26

Noreen walked inside and went straight back to the bathroom off the kitchen, shut the door, and stood looking at her face in the mirror. She turned on the tap and rinsed out her mouth, splashed water on her face. After that she sat on the toilet and pressed her fingers in her hair and leaned forward and looked at her feet, letting worry wash over her in cold waves.

She stood to pull down her pants and have a pee. Sitting on the toilet again, she started to feel very old. Then she looked down at her underpants. There was blood, quite a bit more than there had been the first time. Looking at it made her feel dizzy. The doctor had said some spotting was normal. But was this *some*? How much was too much?

She went upstairs to her room, pulled off her clothes and put on clean underpants and a long white T-shirt and immediately got into bed. She pulled the part of the sheet over her face that still smelled of Wesley, his sweat and aftershave and the deep sweet intoxicating musk of their lovemaking.

Outside the window she heard Dolores say something to Mary, who started to laugh.

"Ahhhh!" Dolores said, her voice rising up through the window. "You believed me!"

"Did not!" said Mary.

"You did! I had you going. Admit it."

Noreen pulled the covers completely over her head, curled up, and shivered. She felt some cramping—just like having a really bad period. So she lay flat out on her back and began to pray. She asked God if She would take care of everything because she, Noreen, certainly couldn't.

Then she began to get a terrible headache, lying in bed and thinking about leaving everything up to God. So she thought about lightning and thunder and rain and the vast sky—imagined floating up into God's arms. God was large and fleshy and as dark as the clouds. God had a beautiful deep voice. She could sing to you and make you lay your burdens down beside your bed and then drift you off to a good place.

After about half an hour Noreen opened her eyes. She had begun to feel a little better. She could hear the comforting sound of talking and laughter coming up from the kitchen, as well as the smell of freshly brewed coffee. Outside the window, a faint breeze brought in the scent of rain. She pulled on her jeans and went downstairs.

They sat around the table in the kitchen—Lynda and Seth, Del, Mary, Dolores. Somebody had brought a cake with pink candles. Lynda looked up at her and smiled a guilty smile.

Seth said, "We were waiting for you. How come you were sleeping?"

Noreen sat down with them and didn't answer. Del reached across the table, lit the candles, and sat back. Dolores started singing "Happy Birthday" and then they all joined in and Lynda blew out her candles.

Noreen got up from the table and went upstairs and picked up her backpack. She found a bunch of change jangling around in the bottom, stuffed it all in her pocket, and went downstairs to the side door.

"Aren't you having cake with us, Pumpkin?"

"I have to go," she said, addressing them all. "I have to do something."

She went out and ran across to Shore's Groceries. It was still early enough that Gladys wouldn't have gone to work yet.

The line was crackling and the phone rang several times. Gladys didn't have an answering machine. On the sixth ring, though, she picked up, out of breath—as if she had been running from somewhere.

"Gladys," said Noreen. "Don't say anything and don't hang up on me even if you are probably mad. I've got some things to explain to you. If you hate me after everything I tell you then that's up to you. But I really need you to listen to me. And I hope I've got enough change here to get through it all."

27

It felt like a funeral at the café when she got back. Everybody still sat around the table as before—except for Seth, who had disappeared—but they were all long-faced and somber. Dolores kept looking at her hands, playing with her rings, letting out the odd sigh. Mary dabbed at her eyes. Delbert, his eyes red, stared at some invisible spot in the room. Lynda's face was blotchy from crying. It wasn't hard to guess what had happened.

Noreen went in search of Seth and then saw him through the screen door, sitting with Tessie on the steps that led into the backyard. He had his arm around the dog, who sat straight and still as a soldier beside him, except to reach around and lick his face. Noreen quietly opened the door and slid outside and sat down next to them.

"This is the most awful day of my life," said Seth, leaning his head against her. "My mom says she's going to shut down the café. If we move I'll have to leave everybody behind, Del and Auntie Dolores and Auntie Mary. And even you. I can't stand it, Noreen."

Tessie moved out into the yard, circled around, head down, then came back and sat by their feet. Noreen put her arms around Seth and held on.

28

It didn't hurt. That was the strange thing. She could not believe a clot that big could slide out of her body. Mary and Del had gone home and Dolores had stayed on to talk to Lynda a little longer. Seth was upstairs, probably sitting comatose in front of the TV. She had gone into the bathroom because something felt wrong again, and now she knew that what was happening wasn't normal. Couldn't be. Then she had to sit down again as two more huge clots came away. Pieces of her baby—she was sure—pieces of Star.

She pulled up her pants and went to the door of the bathroom and opened it. "Something just happened," she said numbly.

Dolores got up so fast, her chair toppled over backward. Lynda stumbled around it and they both crowded into the bathroom.

But it was over and Noreen knew it. There was nothing anybody could do.

She turned to Dolores, who said, "Do you want me to call Wesley?"

"He won't come," said Noreen, her heart finally breaking. "He won't because I sent him away."

"Foolish girl," murmured Dolores, drawing her in, hugging her close, rocking her back and forth. "Of course he'll come. He'd bring down the sky if you asked him to. So tell me his number right now because I'm going to call him up."

Later, an almost half-moon shone over the water and she sat out on Del's deck and looked at the lake, holding fast to its gleam, pulling it inside her.

Wesley, who had arrived within an hour of Dolores's call, tucked her up in blankets and then walked away and came back and walked away again—restlessly pacing between the deck and inside the cottage. Each time he laid his hand on her shoulders, or knelt down and hugged her, or stroked her arm, or kissed her forehead. Then he'd go away for a while.

A party—a strange celebration—was going on around her. For Star. For Lynda's café. Del had gone up to Willow Creek and bought pizza for everybody. He brought a slice out to her and stood by solemnly while she choked it down. At one point he said, "You and your boyfriend can stay here at the cottage tonight. Have some time to yourselves."

Now he reappeared with an ice-cream bar. He pulled back the paper wrapper before handing it to her. "You're young," he offered. "You'll have another baby."

Dolores overheard and snapped, "Stop that, Delbert. That's just the kind of well-meaning talk that drives grief through the heart like a knife."

"I'm sorry," he said, looking like a man who had just committed a terrible crime.

Noreen grabbed his hand and pressed it to her cheek. "I've made such a mess of things," she whispered. "I can't even have a baby right."

He hunkered down beside her. "That's just the way of the world," he whispered back. "It shakes us all, kid."

She leaned in and threw her arms around his neck and smelled the milky trace of pizza cheese and hugged him. He returned her hug—hesitantly at first, but then adding several awkward yet heartfelt thumps to her back.

A thought grew. A creative thought. A powerful thing. What the hell, she figured. I've got nothing left to lose. "Del," she whispered slowly in his ear, "Lynda—is in love with you. Totally. In love with you."

He dropped his arms and lurched back as if she'd sent a lightning bolt through his body. Then he staggered to his feet. Noreen held him in her unwavering gaze. Held him like a goddess in the war of love. Watched as he reeled away and disappeared into the shadows behind the cabin. His truck started up. She listened as he drove away, spinning dirt. Then she turned her face upward to the brilliant starry night.

When they got into bed later, Wesley held her close. "I never got to see it," he whispered. "The heartbeat. Tell me again, what it looked like."

"A pinpoint of light. That flashed," said Noreen.

"That's why it looked like a star?"

"Yes."

"Did it look like it was inside an actual baby?"

"It was hard to tell."

"And it was beautiful."

"It was . . . powerful."

"So now you're not going to have a baby."

Noreen, feeling lonely in his arms, looked up at the ceiling. "No. She's gone." Turning her face on the pillow, she looked at his dark profile for quite a while. Then, "And please don't tell me I can have another one. I wanted *her*. Can you understand that? It feels like there could only have been one of her."

He turned to look at her. "Sort of like her mother."

Early the next morning they went over to the clinic at Willow Point. The doctor on duty was not the same one she had seen the first time.

"It's nothing to worry about," this doctor said. "It's especially common in the first couple of months. Yours could have been some kind of random chromosomal error. Won't affect your ability to have children at another time. But I'd advise you to wait for a while. A long while. Please do yourself that favor. You've got your whole life ahead of you. I get far too many pregnant teenagers coming through here. Most of them, of course, decide not to go through . . ." He stopped, shot at look a Noreen, then at Wesley. "Sorry. Guess in light of your situation that sounds insensitive."

Noreen thought, Yes, it does. But she said instead, "Is that it?"

"Afraid so. You'll need to go for another ultrasound, of course, just to make absolutely sure there's nothing left. No residual tissue."

"The residual tissue, of course, would be what's left of my baby."

"That's right," said the doctor with a startled look.

"Well then, screw it. I don't need to look at some godforsaken empty screen."

Wesley followed her out to the truck. They sat in silence for a long time before he started the engine, backed up, and headed down the highway for Pembina Lake. All the way she wanted to say something to him—about how empty she felt, and how ashamed, and how she didn't know what she could do to make things right in the wake of the mess she had caused for everybody.

Wesley's hand found hers. Their hands connected across the

seat. "Promise me," he said, breaking the silence, "that you'll go back and see that doctor if you have to. Or to somebody else. I don't want to lose you, too."

"You're not losing me, Wesley," she said testily. "I love you, for heaven's sake."

There it was, out in the open. Just as clear as anything. In her distraction and sadness she'd gone and said it. But it felt fine. It felt like a light pressure, like the weight of a wing, had briefly caressed her heart, then lifted and fluttered away.

29

On their way back to the cottage they passed the café. It was all closed up, but Del's truck was parked outside and Del was nowhere to be seen. The light over Lynda's door was still on—like it hadn't been turned off from the night before. Noreen craned her neck as they drove past. She tried to get a glimpse of any movement behind the café window, but she couldn't see a thing. She tried to remember if his truck had been there when she and Wesley had gone by the first time, on their way to the clinic. But she couldn't.

"What's up?" said Wesley.

"I'm not sure," Noreen told him. "Let's just keep going."

She settled back in her seat and they continued along the lakeside road. Pembina Lake, dark green and rolling, cast waves and foam on the shore below. The smell of rain was in the air.

"Crazy weather," said Wesley. He paused. Then, turning to her, he said, "So are you coming back to Brandon to live with me? Since you say you love me? I did hear you right, didn't I?"

"Wesley," Noreen said firmly. "I've got things to think about. Things aren't just all about you, you know."

"I'll take that as a definite maybe then, from a girl who is a real handful," said Wesley, looking down the lake—at the thick mountain-high storm clouds that were boiling toward them from the south.

Halfway to the cottage they discovered Dolores walking along on their side of the road. Seth was with her. They both carried plastic pails spilling over with dark berries. Wesley pulled to a stop and Noreen opened the truck door. "Want a lift?"

Dolores was out of breath. She lifted Seth to Noreen, who grabbed him under the arms and put him on her lap. He scrambled onto her knees. Dolores eased herself up inside and sat down with a grunt, placing the berry pails on the floor by her feet. "Going to be flying out to Prince Edward Island next week," she announced. "With Mary. See her great-grandchild. She didn't want to fly by herself, you know. She's had some health problems that scared her. Anyway . . ." Smoothing the creases in her brown slacks, looking at them both in turn, "Time I had some fun, too. You're never too old, they say. So, Pumpkin—you leaving us?" But she didn't wait for an answer. "You can always come back and visit, you know. We aren't going anywhere. Except, of course, for our stay in the Maritimes. I'm going to eat a lobster. Never had one before in my life. Oh, and here's our stop," she ran on cheerfully. "Looks like rain again. Well, you can help me make those Saskatoon pies, just like a big boy, Seth. Good day for inside work. Hasn't this been the craziest July?"

Wesley pulled to a stop. Dolores swung the door open. Seth was in a hurry and didn't bother saying goodbye. He just slid past them all and hit the ground running and leaping—green shorts and shirt blending with the leaves and the grass and the shadows and the rain that had just begun to fall.

Before she got out, Dolores quickly hugged Noreen and said, "Don't be a stranger, now."

30

In the living room of Del's cottage, Noreen stood looking down at the scorched blue carpet. It really was a mess. In the light of day it was even worse than she remembered.

"So what happened here?" said Wesley, coming up behind her.

"Long story."

He let out a low whistle. "It was you who did this? To the guy's carpet?"

"Yes. I did. So shoot me. I've done lots worse things, Wesley."

She found a red pen in her backpack. She pulled out Del's work reports and flipped through them. There was nothing she had written that would be important for him to see, especially not now. She thought about the light over the door at Lynda's café. It

180

was still on because—just maybe—she had finally managed to do something right in this little town. She tore a blank sheet of paper from the notebook and thought for a minute about all the things she could say. Then she smiled as she carefully drew a big heart. What, really, was left but this?